THE KEY

THE KEY

•

Eric C. Evans

AVALON BOOKS
NEW YORK

PRINTED IN THE UNITED STATES OF AMERICA
ON ACID-FREE PAPER
BY HADDON CRAFTSMEN, BLOOMSBURG, PENNSYLVANIA

For Debora:
Something in the way she moves . . .

I would like to thank Zanne Evans, Yoshie Walbeck, and Kerry Casaday, whose suggestions and editing made all the difference, Stuart Stevens, whose experience and advice have been critical, and particularly Veronica Mixon and Ellen Mickelsen, respectively my editor and publisher at Avalon Books, for the confidence they have shown in my work and the opportunities they have given me.

A special thanks to my wife Debora, who always believed that a guy like me could write a novel. Thankfully, love is, in fact, blind.

Chapter One

I don't know if it was something about that particular morning, or perhaps the resonance of those particular footsteps, but the first sound of her shoe hitting the long wooden deck leading to my trailer startled me from a deep sleep.

It was the last decent sleep I would get for some time.

Throwing off my covers, I rolled out of bed onto my knees and looked out my bedroom window. I had not seen her in nearly twenty years but recognized her immediately. Suzanna Hutton—or Tanner, or whatever her name was after her divorce—was walking toward my trailer as if she owned the place. As she did, she removed a dark pair of sunglasses and shook her head so that her hair fell into place, framing her almost-too-perfect face.

She had knocked on my door twice by the time I found my rarely used bathrobe and made it to the front room of my trailer. I tied the ever-shrinking belt and checked my hair in the reflection of a clock, which hung by my door. It looked so bad I wished I hadn't even bothered to look. Shrugging my shoulders, I opened the door.

"Lafayette Henrie?" She used my whole name the way people in the South sometimes do when they are greeting someone they haven't seen in a long time.

1

"Hello . . . Hi, uh, Suzanna? I'm a little . . . I mean a lot . . ." I stammered.

"Hello. I hope I haven't caught you at an inconvenient time," she said, knowing that she had.

"No, of course not. Please come in, I'll go finish dressing." It was hot for an October morning, and Suzanna was giving a spaghetti-strapped sundress what would undoubtedly be its last wearing of the season.

"Why don't I just wait out here? Do you have time for an early lunch?" she asked after taking a long look around my trailer and not finding it to her taste.

"Sure. You bet. Hang on while I get dressed," I said, scampering back to the bedroom to find some clean clothes.

Every once in a while in life something happens that is so unexpected, so far from the ordinary that the brain, like an overloaded computer, can't process the information. This was one of those times. I had known Suzanna Hutton in high school but just barely. And, likewise, she had barely known me.

That is not to say that I had not kept track of Suzanna. In fact, it was nearly impossible to live in Marianna and avoid knowing the details of her life. But the only sustained conversation she and I ever had was late one night during my sophomore year in high school. My friends and I spotted her by the road with a flat tire. My buddies hated Suzanna, but I insisted they stop and let me help. I was jacking the car up when they drove off, laughing and throwing empty beer cans at us. I finished changing her tire and she gave me a ride home with a very sedate "Thank you." From then on, she always spoke to me when we saw each other, but the friendship was never as warm as I thought it might have been or at least wanted it to be.

She left Marianna as fast as she could after graduation and headed for Emory University in Atlanta. Her father was a well-to-do alumnus and served as one of the school's trustees.

The next time I heard Suzanna's name was nearly eight years later, just as I was made a lieutenant detective in the Atlanta PD. Suzanna married Stansfield Tanner, an ultra-rich Atlanta businessman who, at forty-eight years of age, had decided that his first wife, who had supported him and borne and raised his children while he amassed a staggering fortune, no longer understood him and needed to be replaced. Stansfield, you see, needed a wife with a better understanding of his rightful place in the universe . . . or at least among the Atlanta elite.

The first wife had been divorced and replaced with the younger, more refined Suzanna.

But it was only a few years later—six to be exact—when Stansfield discovered that Suzanna, too, lacked in whatever essential quality that a man of his standing requires. And she, too, was summarily dismissed.

But having been raised in a moderately wealthy family, Suzanna was not intimidated by Stan's money or his bevy of high-priced lawyers. And despite a well-written prenup, she was able to separate Stansfield from a sizable chunk of his money—although I am sure he considered the money mere pocket change. The divorce had just been finalized a few months before, and she had moved into her parents' old house out on the Mill Pond, at least temporarily, while the gossip in the exclusive Atlanta suburb of Buckhead died down. And although Suzanna and I had both lived in Atlanta for at least ten years, our paths had never crossed.

I threw on a blue pullover shirt and a pair of khakis, washed my face, and ran a comb through my hair. Then I joined Suzanna, who was waiting for me in her car.

"Where would you like to eat?" she asked as she pulled onto the highway.

"Truck Stop makes a pretty good hamburger," I suggested, knowing she would hate it.

She glanced at me over the top of her sunglasses and

hesitated for a moment before saying, "Sounds good," and made quick work of getting us there.

The thing that impresses you first about Suzanna is her perfect skin, especially around her prominent cheekbones and deep brown eyes. It is smooth as silk and of the warmest coloring I have ever known. Suzanna, to her credit, lets its natural beauty shine through by wearing only a sparing amount of makeup. Her hair was slightly darker than it had been twenty years ago but still had that alluring shade of natural blond.

As we arrived at the truck stop, she donned an extremely wide-brimmed straw hat, the kind you would expect to see at a garden party in Buckhead.

"You know, I think you're going to make the other truckers jealous if you wear that inside," I said, pointing to the hat.

It took her a second to catch on, but she removed the hat and carelessly tossed it into the backseat of her car without comment.

The metropolis of Marianna, Florida enjoys the distinction of being the only town between Tallahassee and Pensacola deserving of not just one, but two, freeway exits—one on the east end of town and one on the west end. Around the two exits, there are several good-sized truck stops, but this particular one was the first big truck stop built in Marianna and therefore enjoys the distinction of being *The* Truck Stop.

The building is divided into two halves. One half is a store—the kind of store that makes me scared to drive on the interstate. It is filled with a collection of the strangest and most useless knickknacks since the lava lamp. Vintage fruitcakes, a likeness of Elvis in every possible medium, alligators made of pipe cleaners and peanut hulls, Mexican jumping beans, etc. The Elvis stuff is okay, but nobody in their right mind would want any of that other stuff. Yet the people who own this truck stop—or those who own the thousands like it all over the country—manage to make a living selling this stuff. The fact that they can, I'm afraid, does not say much for the collective mental health of interstate travelers.

The other half of the building is a restaurant dominated by a large orange lunch counter and ringed by a row of naugahyde booths so old the vinyl veneer had worn through in many spots.

At Suzanna's request, we took a seat away from the normal crowd, which was clustered around the counter and in the first several booths. I thought this kind of place would make her uncomfortable, but if it did, I couldn't tell by her body language. She took her seat and laid the napkin in her lap.

We had only been seated for a moment when a waitress, whose age could have been anywhere from thirty to sixty, came over to take our order. Trusting that my recommendation would be acceptable, I ordered hamburgers for both of us.

"Tell me what you've been up to since high school," she said after the waitress left.

"Graduated from high school. Did my two years at Chipola Junior College, turned down a job at the prison, went to the University of Florida, graduated in English, moved to Atlanta, worked as a detective in the Atlanta PD. Got shot. Twice. Moved home. Now I spend my days reading, fishing, and collecting disability."

I hadn't added anything to what she must have already known.

"And what do you read?" she asked with a wry smile.

It brought a smile to my face as well. I apologized and said, "I find it hard to believe that we're here to catch up on old times."

"I hope that I haven't offended you, but I did think it appropriate that we catch up before getting immediately down to business. But if you prefer . . ." she said, letting her sentence finish itself.

"If it's all the same to you, let's get the business out of the way first," I suggested as our meals arrived.

"Certainly," she said, and her demeanor changed to that of a businesswoman. "As I'm sure you have heard, Stansfield and I have divorced."

"Yes, I seem to recall reading something about that in the *Floridian,*" I said facetiously.

As if she were proud of her wrecking-ball divorce, she flashed me her first uncontrived smile of the day. I acknowledged my accomplishment with a slight nod.

"Anyway, that's all done now. I hit him where it hurts— in the wallet," she said, as my mind conjured up another, more vivid image.

"It was a glancing blow, as I understand it," I said, wondering what type of reaction I would get.

"If you consider that I shouldn't have gotten a thing, I think I did quite well," she said.

"Everything is relative," I said as the waitress returned to leave the check. Without protest from Suzanna, I slid the check to my side of the table and began dousing my fries with catsup.

"There is only one unsettled issue remaining," Suzanna said when we were alone again.

Not sure what to say, I began to eat my burger and waited for further explanation.

"While Stan and I were on our honeymoon, he gave me—oh, I don't know—several hundred thousand dollars in jewelry that we had bought in Europe. He was concerned about trying to get it through Customs, so we opened a safe-deposit box on the last leg of our trip in Grand Cayman and left it there. We were down there so often, I just left it and used it when we were down there. I had more than enough jewelry at home.

"Now fast-forward six years. About three months before

the divorce, I misplaced the key to the safety deposit box. Or at least I thought I had. I don't know how long it had been gone when I noticed it, but one day I saw it was not in my jewelry box where I had always kept it."

She picked up her fork and studied the tines so intently it almost appeared as if she was talking to it, rather than to me.

"I searched everywhere but couldn't find it," she continued. "That's when I started suspecting that Stan had taken it. By that time it was obvious that things were going bad between him and me. I searched all his stuff, too, but couldn't find the key." She laid the fork back on the table and turned her attention back to me.

"Stan had a small safe in his office—always locked. One night he was out playing cards and I noticed the door to his office was open. It took me more than an hour, but I tried every single number of significance in Stan's life until I finally figured out the combination which, incidentally, was the date of his first divorce, and opened the safe. There it was tucked away with his passport. I took the key and decided to hide it myself.

"Then one day, a few months later, Stan asked me to meet him for lunch, where he told me he had filed for divorce. He presented me with a key to a condominium and told me I could use it while I got my affairs in order. Later that same afternoon, a moving company delivered all my stuff to the condo. Since that day, I have never been allowed back in that house. Well, except once, but Stan's attorney was with me the whole time." She paused and absentmindedly patted her lips with her napkin, even though she still had not taken a bite of her food.

"Not long after the divorce was final, I got a letter from Stan's attorney asking me to return the key. Through my attorney, I wrote back that I did not have the key and, as far as I knew, his client was in possession of the key.

Which, of course, was technically accurate. You see, it
was—it is—still in the house, but it is so well hidden, I'm
sure he'll never find it," she said with the smile you would
expect to find on a newly crowned prom queen.

"About a week later, I get a call from Stan. Sweet as
sugar. 'Honey, I need that key.' When I told him I did not
have the key, the conversation quickly went downhill. I
mean, can you believe it? The man's worth hundreds of
millions of dollars and he's worrying about a few hundred
thousand in diamonds and gold."

I had to chuckle at the way the words "a few hundred
thousand dollars" fell off her lips. Like it wasn't just trivial,
it bordered on disdainful. Our eyes met, and she realized
how that must have sounded to a guy like me. I could see
she thought about trying to explain it away but decided
against it and moved on.

"Anyway, I want the jewelry. My attorney claims that
under the divorce decree and the prenup—what little remained intact after I got done with it—clearly states that
any gifts made to me during the marriage are mine. And
I'm not going to let him have them."

By the look on her face, I could tell that she was past
worrying about how selfish she sounded, so I simply asked,
"And this has what to do with me?"

"I need to get that key," she said, as she carefully lifted
the bun of her hamburger, using only her thumb and index
finger, and looked underneath.

"Yes?" I said, still having no clue what exactly she
wanted from me.

"I need someone who can get the key for me."

"Isn't that how your lawyer earns his money?" I asked.

"Don't you see? Stan thinks I've got the key. If he finds
out he's got the key, no court in the land is going to keep
him from taking that stuff. American courts have no juris-
diction down there, and I sure can't keep him from taking

it," she said after finishing her inspection and pushing the hamburger toward the middle of the table.

"I still don't know what you want from me," I said, even more confused.

"I want you to get the key," she said flatly.

"How can I— Oh, no, you've got the wrong guy. Are you crazy?" I said, dropping what was left of my last few fries and pushing myself away from the table as though it would somehow dissociate me from the whole situation.

"You'll be in and out in less than two minutes. And he'll never know; he already thinks I have the key!" she said, her brown eyes pleading with me.

"If it's that easy, why don't *you* go get it?" I said.

"One of the first embarrassments Stan heaped on me was a restraining order. Imagine the great Stansfield Tanner needing protection from me. He knew he had nothing to fear from me, he just wanted to show me what I was up against. I guess he thought it would scare me. He thought wrong. Anyway, any time I am even spotted in that neighborhood, he can have me thrown in jail. And believe me, he would get great pleasure out of seeing me in jail. You, on the other hand, can move in and out of that neighborhood and never raise even the slightest suspicion."

"Suzanna, I'm flattered that after not speaking to each other for twenty years, when you needed someone to pull a black-bag job, you immediately thought of me. But I'm not interested. I'll find my own way home," I said and got up to leave.

She reached across the table and grabbed my hand. "Hank, listen to me, please. The jewelry is mine, the key is mine, and until a few months ago, the house was at least part mine. This is only wrong in the narrowest sense. And I'll pay you fifty thousand dollars cash for your trouble."

"Why me?" I asked, trying not to show that my interest level had now climbed considerably above zero.

"One, I want to be able to trust absolutely that whoever

gets the key doesn't take anything else. There are a lot of valuable things in the house. Two, although you're not a criminal, I think your police background probably gives you the expertise to pull this off. And three, if something does happen, the combination of your contacts and relationships with the law enforcement types and the innocuous nature of what we're doing . . ." She stopped in mid-sentence, wishing she had not brought up the third point.

But she had two good points. Well, three if you counted the money.

"Listen, my answer is no," I said, looking into her eyes so that she would understand that I meant it. "If I change my mind, I'll call you."

Chapter Two

I was shot twice in the line of duty while a member of the Atlanta PD. The first and least serious time had been my fault. The second and nearly fatal time had been my partner's fault. It ended both our careers. Mine because I could not get a medical clearance, his because no one trusted him to back them up. Funny how things work out. He is now chief of security for a downtown Atlanta bank, making at least three times as much as he would ever have made on the force. Meanwhile, I was laid up in the hospital for weeks with a shattered vertebra, thinking I might never walk again. Decorated for valor—the whole nine yards—and I am barely keeping body and soul together on disability income.

I hung around Atlanta for a while during my recovery, but all my friends there were cops. They were all very good to me and at first went out of their way to stay in touch and keep me involved, but it was inevitable that we would grow apart. As time passed I got fewer and fewer visits from them. New cops were hired, old ones were transferred or moved on to less stressful careers. So even though Atlanta is the home of the love of my life—the Braves—I decided it was time to leave. (Besides, TBS carries almost all the Braves games live, and I can't afford my season tickets anymore anyway.) That decision being made, there was really no other place for me to go but home—Marianna, Florida.

Most people hold a special feeling for the place of their nativity, and in that way I am no different than most people. Situated in the northwest corner of Florida, about fifteen miles from Alabama and twenty miles from Georgia, Marianna is no more nor less unique than most small towns I have ever been in. The people are down-to-earth and friendly, churches and schools serve as cultural nerve centers, and there is at least one of everything you might need to hold you over until the next trip out to Panama City, Tallahassee, or Dothan, Alabama. Unless, of course, you have a massive coronary. In that case you may run into a problem. My family is under strict instructions from my father that if he ever suffers from such a fate we aren't to waste a moment with the Jackson County Hospital. Saying he "would rather take his chances on the road," our orders are to take him directly to Flowers Hospital in Dothan.

Marianna is much more Southern than Floridian, but therein lies its uniqueness. Though you could spend hours, days, weeks, or even months in Marianna and not know it, you are no more than an hour's drive from the prettiest beaches the Gulf Coast has to offer.

When I decided to leave Atlanta, I sold my small house in Doraville (a place that a favorite band of mine aptly describes as "a touch of country in the city") for little more than I was expecting. I put my windfall in the bank thinking it might someday make a good down payment on a house if I were to ever get back on my feet—financially speaking—again.

When the time came to make the move to Marianna, I thought for half a second about moving in with my parents for a while, but dismissed that idea before it had even finished forming in my mind. Instead, I rented a small apartment on Putnam Street, not far from what passes for downtown Marianna. I had been living there for about three months when Willie Free stopped by for what had become one of his regular visits.

"Got time to take a ride with me?" he asked as he tried but failed to suppress a smile.

"Willie, you've managed to ask me for the only thing I have enough of to give anyway—time," I said as I closed my door and followed him to his car.

Willie and I had been friends since the first day of kindergarten. There was no one in our class with a last name that began with "G," so when our teacher sat us in alphabetical order Willie and I were desk mates. We were never best friends but had always been close. There was a connection between us that kept us involved in each other's lives. We didn't exchange Christmas cards or go out of our way to stay in touch, but our friendship was not like that— it did not need any superficial gestures to survive and thrive. While I had lived in Atlanta, he had lived in Birmingham, and we went for several years at a time without any contact at all. In fact, for several years I didn't even know how to get in touch with him.

After high school Willie was heavily recruited to play basketball and football in colleges all over the country. He finally decided to follow his father's footsteps to play football at Florida A&M University where, owing to his chiseled features and statuesque frame, he became known, much to his chagrin, as the Black Adonis. As fate would have it, though, he was a step too slow for the NFL, so after graduating he moved on to Florida State University Law school.

After law school, he accepted a job at a large law firm in Birmingham. He worked his way up the hourly billing food chain until about two years ago when he made a pretty decent score on a class action lawsuit of some kind. After that he cashed in, moved back to Marianna, hung out his shingle, and now spends more time fishing and golfing and less time pursuing justice. Willie doesn't talk about his work very much, but he did tell me one time that he makes most of his money now by consulting with other attorneys on class action lawsuits. It must not be a bad way to make a living; it doesn't seem to require much of his time.

"Where we headed?" I asked as he drove toward the east end of town.

"Got a place I want to show you," he said. "You know I've been on the board at the bank for the last two years." There are several banks in Marianna, but when people say "the bank" they are usually referring to the Bank of Marianna.

"I didn't know that. Doesn't that cut into your golfing time?" I said.

"It does, but they've been good to give money to my church, you know, sponsoring choir trips and that kind of thing. And from time to time, I'm able to help my friends . . . like I'm about to help you," he said. I smiled, though I had no idea what he had in mind. I knew something about Willie that his legal adversaries would never guess in a million years—Willie had a big heart. I also knew that something his legal adversaries often complained about was also fundamentally true—Willie was a showman. So I didn't ask any more questions as he drove me to a dirt road off Magnolia Road and then onto a two-trail road. The two-trail road twisted and turned for a few hundred yards through trees and underbrush before it eventually opened up into an acre-wide clearing. It was banked on one side by the Chipola River and on the other by Dry Creek, which emptied into the river. The clearing was dotted liberally with large oak and tall pine trees, and in the middle of the clearing sat a beat-up, singlewide trailer.

"Can't say much for the trailer, but the rest of it is a little slice of heaven," I said as we got out of the car.

"Hadn't been kept up that good," Willie said, pointing to a thick stand of weeds around the trailer. There were several old car parts strewn around the place and a surprising amount of trash left by boaters stopping by to picnic on their way down the river.

"No, but that stuff's all superficial. Underneath you can tell this place is beautiful," I said.

"I thought you'd see it that way. I bought it from old Slappy Martin's widow so the bank wouldn't have to foreclose on her," he said with his back toward me, as if what he were saying were wholly unimportant.

"That was nice of you," I said in kind.

"Oh, I didn't do it to be nice," he said, turning to face me. "It's a good investment, don't you think?"

"If you got it at a good price, it could be," I said.

"Trouble is, to make it pay off, I have to either spend a lot more money on it—Sharita would kill me if I did that—or spend a lot of time working on it myself. And that would cut into my golf time. I know you'll understand when I say that option is equally unacceptable," Willie said with the characteristic flair of a trial lawyer.

"I see your dilemma," I said, playing along.

"Yes. So my proposal is this—and believe me it would be a big favor—I want you to take this place off my hands." He held up his hand to keep me from saying anything and continued. "Hear me out, I know they've got you on a fixed income, but I think we can work out a payment plan that will work for both of us."

"Willie, you know I can't borrow that much money from you. How much did you pay for it, anyway?"

"I only had to pay about twenty-seven thousand dollars. What about if I help you get the loan from the bank?"

"Twenty-seven thousand? That's all?" I said in dismay.

"That's it," he said with a smile, seeing that he had me hooked.

"Willie, I can't borrow that much money from you, and I won't borrow it from the bank either. But I will pay you cash for it," I said.

The fact that I had that much cash shocked Willie, who was not certain if I was joking or not.

"Had that much left over when I sold my house in Atlanta," I said, answering Willie's next question before he had a chance to ask it.

"It's a deal then?" he said, extending his hand for a shake.

"It's a deal," I said as I grabbed his hand.

"That trailer livable?" I asked.

"Depends on what you mean by livable. Got running water and the power's hooked up. Let's take a look," he said as we started walking toward my new home.

I spent the next few months getting the place cleaned up and the trash hauled off. Late one night, after my father was safely tucked into bed, my mother gave me his old John Deere riding lawn mower. It took me about a week and two hundred and fifty dollars in parts to get the thing running again. And once I did, it almost destroyed my back before I could get the place mowed.

My next renovation was to build a dock out on the river. I had just enough money, after paying Willie, to buy the wood I needed and to pay a man to set the posts in the riverbed for me. I did the rest of the work myself. I bought some lawn chairs and sat out on the dock every evening that the gnats and mosquitoes would let me, reading or just watching the sunset. After that I went a little overboard. The dock looked strange just sitting out there by itself, so I built a small boardwalk from it to the front door of the trailer. And then that, too, looked strange, so I built a deck around the front door, which connected to the boardwalk. It was perfect, and that's where I should have stopped. But, of course, I didn't. I decided what the place really needed was another boardwalk from the deck to the place my driveway ended. So I built boardwalk out that way too.

The day I finished, I was sitting out on the deck late in

the evening when Willie drove up. He got out of his Explorer and looked at my handiwork for several minutes without a word.

"If your deck is worth more than your trailer, you might be a redneck," he finally said with considerable satisfaction.

My only defense was to laugh—I knew it was true.

At 5:30 every Friday morning there comes a loud knock on my bedroom window. The Friday after my meeting with Suzanna was no exception.

"Lafayette, get your lazy self outta bed and let's go fishing." As always, it was Willie, who, unlike Suzanna, somehow manages to get all the way up to my bedroom window without waking me. Since returning to Marianna, Willie has been the choir director at Poplar Hills Baptist Church, and take my word for it, there is nothing more jarring than his booming voice at 5:30 in the morning.

"All right, all right. I'll be out in a minute. Just shut up," I said, struggling out of bed and into my fishing clothes.

Five minutes later, we had picked up some coffee from the store and were headed east on Highway 90 toward Lake Seminole. In a state where the highest elevation commands the height of 364 feet, it is hard to find places to put dams, but just west of the town of Chattahoochee along the Chattahoochee River they found just such a place.

The Jim Woodruff Dam was one of three built during the late 1940s and early 1950s so that the Apalachicola, the Chattahoochee, and the Flint Rivers could be more easily navigated. Its main function today is providing hydropower to surrounding businesses and homes. But the main resource it provides—as far as I'm concerned anyway—is some very good fishing.

Lake Seminole, which was created as result of the dam, is a beautiful lake that straddles the Florida/Georgia state line in an area which has been populated by humans for over ten thousand years. Unfortunately, the politicians and

bureaucrats got their bony fingers around the lake and insisted that people with only a Florida fishing license stay
on the Florida side of the lake and, in return, those inter-
loping Georgia fishermen must stay on their side of the
lake. So, fishing on Lake Seminole can be a test of one's
skills in international diplomacy. But when the fish are bit-
ing, take my word for it—it is well worth the effort.

By 6:15, we were on the lake and wondering where all
the fish were hiding—on the Georgia side, no doubt. We
exchanged chitchat for a while, and then I said, "I need
your advice on something, Willie."

"My advice is always free to you," he said without taking
his eyes off his cork.

"I think I need to retain you as my attorney first," I said.

He cocked an eyebrow. "Who you going to sue?"

"I'm not suing anybody. I want your advice, and I want
it protected by the lawyer client privilege."

"I usually don't work while I fish, but in this case, I'm
going to make an exception. Consider me your attorney."

"All right," I said, and went back to fishing. But Willie
was no longer interested in the brim and shellcracker that
were finally starting to nibble at our bait. I had his undi-
vided attention.

"You'll never guess who showed up on my doorstep yesterday morning," I said.

"Who?" he asked, letting me know that he had no interest in guessing.

"Suzanna Hutton, or Tanner, or whatever her last name
is now."

"I believe it is still Tanner. What did she want with
you?" His tone suggested that he couldn't believe she
would have any business with the likes of me.

"She needs some help."

"From you?"

"Yes from me, is that so hard to believe?"

"What did she want?" he asked, ignoring my question.

I told him about the divorce and the safety-deposit box and what she wanted me to do. He stared at me for at least a minute before saying, "I can't believe we're even having this conversation."

"Hold on, Willie. I didn't say I was going to do it," I said, holding my hand up as if I was being falsely accused.

"No, but you're thinking about it. Or we wouldn't be having this conversation. It's stupid, Hank. Why would you even consider a thing like that?" he asked, pointing his finger at me.

"She said she'd pay me fifty thousand dollars."

"Oh, so now you are a professional criminal. That it?"

"Calm down, Willie. That's a lot of money to me."

"That's a lot of money to anybody, except maybe Suzanna. But, as both your attorney and your friend, my strongest possible advice is to drop this whole thing immediately. I could go on all morning with reasons why this is a bad idea. You want me to get started?"

"No. I got it, let's just fish," I said, wishing I had never brought it up.

I had asked Willie his advice, not because I didn't know how he would react, but because I wanted him to talk me out of doing it. Ever since my lunch with Suzanna, I felt like I had inescapably entered her fifty thousand dollar gravitational pull. Though I struggled mightily, I could not escape it. With every thought, it tugged me closer and closer. And the closer I got, the more power it had over me. Against every bit of logic I could summon, I continued to consider Suzanna's offer.

It really wasn't stealing, I told myself. She owned the key and the box. And it was, in my view, reasonable to assume that, given the chance, Stan would steal the jewelry from her. The only remaining problem was the break-in, and there was no way around that one. As a detective, I had on occasion broken into places I was not supposed to be. Nothing major, of course. From time to time, if I needed a little help making a case, I would jimmy a lock to some guy's office, or whatever, and see what I could find that would be helpful. This really wasn't any different than that. Was it?

Late that Saturday afternoon, I called Suzanna and made plans to have dinner.

Chapter Three

It was about 6:00 when I jumped into my Jeep and headed out to the Mill Pond. Suzanna's was a plantation-style home without the plantation. Jackson County, like almost all counties in the Southeast, is sprinkled with plantation houses dating back to before the Civil War. Like many of these grand old homes, Suzanna's had been built in the 60s—the only difference being that hers was constructed in the 1960s and not the 1860s. Indeed, Suzanna's house could not be distinguished from those older homes, even though it was at least a century younger.

It was a large white structure with huge columns and an oak-lined driveway. Above the front door was a second-story porch, onto which Suzanna stepped after I turned into her long tree-lined driveway. She was wearing her hair down and still putting on a pair of earrings as she watched me drive up.

I hate parking in front of a house like this one, especially in my 1975 Jeep. There is nowhere to park, and anywhere you do looks woefully out of place, like a hired hand that hasn't yet been shown to the servants parking area. I parked as near as I could to the front door and jumped out.

"Is this okay?" I asked, looking up to where Suzanna was standing.

"That's fine," she said, wholly unconcerned. "Just come on in. I'll be down in a second. There's some iced tea in the fridge."

I walked in the front door and was greeted by a foyer large enough to park my trailer in during the next hurricane. I had no idea where to find the kitchen, so I wandered around the first floor until I found it at the rear of the house overlooking a meticulously manicured lawn, which abruptly surrendered to the Mill Pond's mossy waters and cypress stumps.

I found the tea and helped myself to a tall glass. I wondered why it was taking Suzanna, who had been completely dressed, so long to come down. Another ten minutes passed before she entered through a door which I had not even noticed, wearing a completely different outfit than she had on when I arrived.

"I'm sorry to keep you, but those jeans didn't hang right. You know what I mean?" she asked.

I suppressed a chuckle and nodded as if I understood exactly what she was talking about.

"Where are we going?" she asked.

"I was thinking about Grady's," I said with a hopeful look on my face.

"That sounds good to me, but I am not riding all the way over to Graceville in a Jeep with no top," she said.

Ten minutes later, I was behind the wheel of her car. I normally go to Graceville through Cottondale. That evening, I decided to catch Highway 2 in Campbellton and take it into Graceville. It takes only a little longer but provides a more scenic drive.

Within forty-five minutes, we were sitting in Grady's waiting room on either side of a beat-up checkerboard with a mismatched set of checkers, exchanging small talk over the noise of a window-mounted air conditioner, which was obviously giving its all to keep the waiting room bearably cool.

Grady's is one of those fabled greasy spoons of which you hear so much but find so few of. Founded decades ago by Grady himself, the restaurant is now run by Grady's grandchildren and is revered by people who know it as the best fried shrimp to be found anywhere along the Gulf Coast.

Grady's is a very temperamental place, which insists on maintaining a very small dining room with an adjoining waiting room at least twice as large. They don't hesitate to close for weeks or even months at a time. But once you taste the deep-fried shrimp, the inconveniences endured seem trivial. Like Pavlov's dogs, you even begin to enjoy the difficult experience of getting them.

Once seated, we ordered and were served our dinner salads, which amounted to not much more than a handful of iceberg lettuce, two tomato wedges, and a third of a cup of dressing. Not being much of a salad person in any case, I left mine untouched, while Suzanna picked through hers for the freshest lettuce.

"I've been thinking about your problem," I said when I was completely out of small talk.

"Yes," she said, trying to look desperate. I wondered if she had even known a feeling of true desperation.

"Tell me a little bit about this place. Where the key is," I said.

"Well, it is a huge house, but the key is easy to find." She retrieved a pen from her purse and grabbed a napkin to draw a map.

"No. I mean how do you know it will be empty? Does it have a security system? That kind of stuff," I said.

"Oh. First of all, Stan doesn't make a move I don't hear about. Trust me," she said as she patted my hand. "And yes, the house does have a security system, quite a sophisticated one. But I can tell you how to disarm it."

"I'm sure he changed the codes the minute he kicked you out," I said.

"Please, Hank, I'm not an idiot," she said, making no attempt to hide the fact that I had offended her. "Let's just say Stan does not inspire a lot of loyalty in those who work closely with him," she said with a sly smile.

I wanted to ask her about those people and how exactly she got Stan's security codes, but decided against it.

"How do you know this information is reliable?" I asked instead.

"I assure you it is absolutely accurate. No doubt at all." I didn't know if she was lying or not, but she certainly sold it well.

"If these people—whoever they are—are so helpful and reliable, why don't you just have them get the key for you?" I said.

"Believe me, I have thought about it. I considered every possible angle, and if there was a way to get that key— other than this"—she waved her hand between use—"I would do it. But this is the best way. For everybody concerned." And since, if I decided to help her out, it would triple my current annual income, I could not argue with her.

We both took a break from the business conversation when our dinners arrived. Twelve large shrimp, battered and deep fried to an amber hue, complimented by fries and a tartar sauce made with dill rather than sweet pickles. There is no garnish, nor even any steamed vegetables, with which to salve a conscience pained by the guilt of eating a dinner comprised entirely of deep-fried foods.

On the drive back to Marianna, we discussed some of the logistics that would be involved.

"Monday night is the time to do it. Stan has a standing card game at the Georgia Club in Atlanta. He's never home before one-thirty, and if he's winning, it's more like three-thirty. Bessie, the live-in maid, has the day off, and she always spends it in Macon with her grandchildren. She gets in Tuesday morning about ten-thirty," Suzanna explained.

"What about when he's out of town? Wouldn't it be better to do it then?" I asked.

"He does travel a lot, but those trips are planned and canceled at a moment's notice. There's no way to plan on them. I'm telling you, Monday night is the time. I'd do it about 10:00 P.M. He will have been gone for at least two hours by then, but it's not late enough to cause a lot of suspicion if anybody sees you."

When we got to her house we went in, and she wrote down, in detail, the directions to the security alarm over another glass of tea at her kitchen table.

"Now for the key," she said. "In my bedroom—Stan and I had adjoining bedrooms—is a four-poster bed. At the tip of each post is a wooden ball about twice as big as your fist," she said, holding up her clenched fists as a visual.

"These balls are screwed onto the post. I took one of our steak knives and hollowed out the top of of one of those balls just enough that I could wedge the key into it and still screw it onto the bed. He will never find it."

"How hard is the bedroom to find?" I asked, pouring myself another glass of tea.

"Oh, it's easy," she said. She left the room briefly and returned with a legal pad and pencil.

"You enter from the door facing the garage," she said as she drew the floor plan on the pad. "Disarm the security system, walk through the mudroom, through the service kitchen, into the dining room, out the south door into a living room, and down the hall to the fourth door. That's it. In and out in less than two minutes." She dropped the pencil on the paper and looked at me.

I had not yet committed to getting the key and was now facing the moment of decision. The kitchen, which had a twelve-foot ceiling and was at least twice as long as it was wide, was dark except for the light that hung over the table. It was silent except for the bullfrogs and crickets along the Mill Pond.

In order to buy more time, I picked up the map she drew and studied it. For her part, Suzanna played it perfectly. She did not say a word. She sensed that anything she said at this point would just make it easier for me to turn her down.

I felt like Rudyard Kipling's Baloo as Kaa performed The Dance of the Hunger of Kaa. I was unable to resist Suzanna's allure. Willingly I stepped into it.

After about five minutes I dropped the pad and said, "I'll do it. But I want half the money up front."

She just smiled and left the room without a word. Not two minutes later she was back with an oversized envelope, which she dropped on the table in front of me with a thud that even John D. Rockefeller would have loved.

Chapter Four

My plan was to leave Marianna at about 5:00 P.M., giving me plenty of time to drive up to Atlanta and arrive at Stan's about 10:00, do the deed, and drive straight back to Marianna.

At about 2:00 that afternoon, I took my Jeep in to be serviced and rented a car for the drive to Atlanta. I dropped by McDonald's for a quick burger, drove out to my place again to pick up the Jimmy Buffett tapes I had forgotten, and was on my way a few minutes after 5:00. I jumped on Highway 231 to Dothan, then I took Highway 431 north through Eufaula into Phenix City, where I crossed over the Chattahoochee River into Columbus, Georgia. I took I-185 to I-85 into Atlanta and got off on the Peachtree Road exit at about 9:30 P.M. I stopped and got some gas, a Dr. Pepper, and a package of cheese crackers at a gas station near the interstate, then drove to the Lenox Square Mall. Finding a secluded area of the parking lot, I used one of those battery-powered screwdrivers to remove the license plate from the car, figuring that if anyone spotted it, they would have no way of linking the car to me without a license plate. On my way out, I would simply remount the tag and be on my way.

At 10:30, I was outside the residence of Stansfield Tan-

27

ner and parked under the dark shadows of an old magnolia tree and a huge azalea bush. The house was big, but not as large as I had imagined, and completely dark except for a row of lights on either side of the driveway and a few lights around the front door. I looked around the neighborhood, which was mostly quiet and seemed to be settling in for the night. I waited for about thirty minutes. Everything remained quiet.

I had planned on knocking at the front door and if by any chance someone answered the door, just say I was lost and ask for directions back to I-85. But assuming no one answered, I would go back to the side door to enter the house. With the lights shining on the front door and none on the side door, I decided to avoid the front door completely. I knocked on the wood-frame side door as loudly as I could and rang the doorbell, waited a minute or so, and tried again. No answer and no one stirring in the house that I could notice.

I used a lock-picking set I had pilfered from the evidence room of the Atlanta PD years before. It took me about thirty seconds to pick the lock. I turned the knob, and the door opened to silence. I did not realize why at first, but it bothered me that the house was so quiet. Not a peep. Nothing. The house was dark, the only light I could see was the moonlight shining in through a large window in the service kitchen. Then it hit me: the security alarm. It wasn't beeping its warning, waiting on me to punch in the proper code to disarm it before it called the police. I could see the alarm from where I stood in the doorway, the green light flashing "not ready," which, according to Suzanna, meant that the alarm was not armed. Nor could it be, because one or more of the doors were open. Was it possible that Stan had left without turning on his alarm? I was pondering that question when I noticed something even more disturbing. The kitchen was a mess. Not the kind of mess when you leave the dinner dishes untouched as you rush out the door to a card game. No. All the cabinets had been opened and emptied, none of the drawers were in the cabinets, the countertops were completely clear. Everything was piled in one huge heap in the middle of the room.

Right then and there, before I had ever set one foot into the house, I should have turned around and gone back to my poor but stress-free life in Marianna. But the cop in me could not resist taking a look around. Like driving by a bad accident on the interstate—I had to take a look.

I walked slowly into the kitchen. With each step, bits of glass and china were crunching under my feet. Nothing in the kitchen had been left untouched. Everything—everything—was in the pile in the middle of the room. Even the potted plants, which had probably been sitting on the windowsill, had been uprooted and thrown with their pots into the pile.

I walked through the kitchen and into the formal dining room; it, too, was similarly trashed. The paintings that had once been on the walls lay on the top of a heap of china, crystal, and overturned dining room furniture.

I walked through the family rooms and checked every room along the hallway to Suzanna's bedroom. Nothing had been left untouched. Everything in the house had been systematically searched and most of it destroyed.

Suzanna's room had not been spared. The bed had been overturned, and the contents of her closet, her towels, the chest of drawers, paintings, photographs—all were heaped on top of her overturned bed, the mattress sliced open in several places and its stuffing strewn all over the room. After donning a pair of rubber gloves, I managed to lift the bedpost high enough off the floor with one hand so that I could unscrew the ball at the top of the post with my other hand. Because I didn't want to move anything from where it lay, I was straining against the entire contents of the room as I twisted the ball. Finally, it came free and there, wedged into the hole, just as Suzanna had said, was a small brass key. I removed the key and put it in my pocket.

Instead of leaving by the same route I had used to find Suzanna's room, I decided to go through the other door in the bedroom to what I was sure from Suzanna's map would be Stan's room.

Of course, the first thing I noticed was the mess. But the second thing I noticed was instantly and permanently etched in my brain. I spent four years as a homicide detective, but I had never in my life seen anything like the lifeless body of Stansfield Tanner. Tied to a small wooden chair, the body appeared to be staring right at me—through me. Although my memory of that scene is so vivid I could describe it in detail, I'll let this suffice: at Stan's funeral the casket was closed.

Chapter Five

I beat the fastest retreat I could from the house, my heart racing and my pulse pounding. I started the car and exerted all my willpower to keep from speeding away as fast as my rental would take me.

The streets of Buckhead were still and quiet as I drove out. After finding Peachtree Road again I began looking for a pay phone. I found one at the Peachtree Battle Shopping Center just as I was about to leave Buckhead.

I almost dialed 911 but remembered that all those calls are recorded. I thought for a moment and then decided to call a number at the Atlanta PD which I believed would not be taped.

"Atlanta PD, Sgt. Wilson," a younger woman's voice said after several rings.

"I need to report a break-in and a murder," I said, relieved that I had no idea who I was talking to.

"Who am I speaking with?" she asked, with the same inflection you hear when the Domino's Pizza guy asks, "Sausage or pepperoni?"

"It's at 333 Knollwood Lane," I said and hung up.

I could not decide what to do next. I wanted to call Suzanna. But a call to Suzanna's home from a pay phone in Buckhead right after her ex-husband had been murdered would not go unnoticed. For that matter neither would a call from my mobile phone routed though a cell tower somewhere in Atlanta.

I knew, of course, that she would be a suspect.

I did not want to hang around the pay phone any longer than I had to, so I got in my car and headed again toward I-85 south. I stopped at the Metro station on Ponce de Leon just off West Peachtree and made a phone call I didn't want to make.

Willie picked up the phone on the second ring.

"Hello."

"Willie, I am sorry to be calling so late. Did I wake you?"

"Don't worry about it, we're just watching Barry White on Letterman. What's up?"

"Well, I'm in Atlanta."

"You didn't tell me—" He stopped in mid-sentence when he realized what I was up to, and I could picture him bolting straight up in his bed.

"You better not be doing what I think you're doing. You are. Aren't you?" he said.

"Just listen to me, Willie—"

"No, you're the one that needs to listen. Hang on while I change phones," he said and slammed the phone down on his nightstand before I could say another word.

There was a pause while I waited for him to pick up again.

"All right, baby, I got it," I heard him say as he picked up a different phone. "All right, do I need to come bail you out of jail?"

"No. Not yet anyway," I said, and explained what had happened at Tanner's house.

"Where are you now?"

"I'm at a pay phone downtown," I said.

"You're lucky my foot can't reach your rear, and the next time it can, you better watch out."

"I'll deserve it, too," I said. "But here is what I'm worried about. Suzanna may be in some kind of danger, too. It was clear that whoever did this was looking for something in that house. And I'm willing to bet they didn't find it."

"Why do you say that?" he said, the anger subsiding in his voice—slightly.

"It was pretty systematic how they did it. Looked to me like they went through the house one room at a time. And as near as I could tell they did the whole house. If they had found what they were looking for, they would have stopped. Don't you think?" I asked.

"I don't know, because unlike you, I don't have experience in breaking-and-entering."

"Yeah, yeah. Listen, call Suzanna, and tell her to be careful. I'll be back to her place about three-thirty or four," I said.

"What if she was in on the murder?" he said flatly.

Willie had given voice to a thought that had been lurking in my subconscious since the moment I saw Stan Tanner's lifeless body.

"Oh, come on Willie, why would she have him killed?" I asked.

"Have you taken a hard blow to the head, Hank? She's got a thousand reasons to want him dead."

"But why send me in right after the murder to get some key?"

"I don't know, maybe you're being set up," he said.

"If that's true, it's the stupidest setup I've ever seen. There are a hundred ways to link me back to her. She's already given me twenty-five thousand dollars in cash. If she's setting me up, she's the stupidest murderer I have ever seen. And I've known a lot of them."

"True enough, but neither you nor I have thought this thing all the way through, and there may be a lot of things—important things—we don't know. Maybe she's going to say she hired you to get the key and killing him was all your idea. It's risky, but with a good lawyer it might work," he said.

"I don't have time to worry about this right now, but if she's not involved, she might be in danger," I said.

"Yeah, so?" he said.

"Maybe you could ride out there and keep an eye on her place until I get there," I said.

"Why don't I just call the police and let them do it?" he asked.

"Listen, Willie, this may all amount to nothing as far as Suzanna is concerned. I don't want to be sucked into this thing if I don't have to be. And if you call the police, then I am right smack dab in the middle of it," I said.

"All right, I'll ride out there and keep an eye on things, but if anything happens, I've got to call the cops," he said, with a long sigh.

"Thank you. You sure you don't mind?" I asked, before I could suck the words back into my mouth.

" 'Course I mind. But what else can I do? Just go back to bed. Some folks are a lot more trouble than they're worth. I'll see you when you get there," he said, and hung up before I had a chance to say another word.

I was back on I-85 driving past Summer Hill when I glanced into my rearview mirror and saw a police car following me. I tried to remain calm, but I had been being careful not to speed, so I knew that could not be it. He continued to follow me for a mile or two, and I had convinced myself that he was just driving down the road, uninterested in me. I decided to test my theory by making a casual lane change.

He followed me and flipped on his lights. For one irrational second I considered trying to outrun him, but I knew that was futile. My mind was racing as fast as my heart. I knew I wasn't speeding, and I could not think of why he would be pulling me over. I changed lanes again and pulled slowly onto the shoulder.

I rolled down my window and waited. Slowly, the officer approached my car with one hand on his pistol and the other holding a flashlight, which he shined into my car and then into my face.

"License and registration," he said when he finally got to my window.

I reached into my wallet, removed my license, found the registration in the glove box, and handed them to the twenty-something police officer.

He carefully examined both before asking, "Mr. Henrie, why are you operating this vehicle without a license plate?"

The relief on my face was surely detectable, even though I was squinting through the light he continued to shine in my eyes.

"As you can see from the registration, this is a rental. I don't know why it's not on the car," I said, as I retrieved the plate from the backseat where I had put it earlier that evening.

"It was in the back window," I continued to lie. "But it fell out when I slammed on the breaks to miss a raccoon."

"A raccoon, huh?"

"Yeah, a raccoon," I said, feeling stupid.

There was a long silence while he was deciding what to do with me.

"You got a screwdriver in there?" he asked, shining his light around the inside of my car again.

At the last possible chance, I stopped myself from saying, "Yes," figuring that having a screwdriver in a rental car would lend credibility to any suspicion he might have that I was the one who removed the plates.

"No, I'm sorry, I don't," I said, shrugging my shoulders.

"Okay. Here's what we're going to do. I'll lend you a screwdriver and you'll do these Rent-a-Wreck people a favor by putting their tag on for them. While you do that,

I'll run your license and this tag. If everything's like it ought to be, we'll let it go at that."

"Sounds good to me," I said.

As I got out of the car, he walked back to his trunk to get a screwdriver. A light rain started to fall as I waited, and I couldn't help but notice the smile on the officer's face as he handed me the screwdriver and withdrew to his car.

By the time I started putting in the last screw, the rain was pouring down. Within a matter of minutes, enough water had collected on the road so that each car that passed doused me as well. I finished the chore as fast as I could and returned to my car. As I did, the officer approached my window. I opened it just enough for him to slide in my license and registration.

"Everything looks good. Drive carefully, and watch out for those raccoons," he said with more than a little sarcasm in his voice.

The relief was overwhelming, and I was even beginning to chuckle, thinking that at least he had also gotten wet. But then I noticed, as he walked back to his car, that he was now wearing a raincoat and showercap-like protector over his hat. Noticing that I was still staring at him, he brought a two-finger salute to the brim of his hat and smiled as if to say, "You're the dummy not me."

I was almost to Newnan, Georgia, before my heart slowed to a normal rate. I could not believe how stupid I had been. Now, all the care I had taken not to leave any trace of my visit to Atlanta was destroyed. Not only had I left a trace, there was now a record of me driving around the city without a license plate and using a threadbare excuse of "slamming on the brakes to miss a raccoon." I knew it was a pretty long jump from there to any kind of a link between me and Stan Tanner's murder, but what other mistakes had I made? In my mind, I went over everything I had done since leaving Marianna. Over and over, I replayed it in my mind. But I couldn't come up with anything.

Yet I couldn't help thinking that there was something that I was overlooking.

Chapter Six

I drove back to Marianna close enough to the speed limit that I would not draw any further attention. Even after the three-and-a-half-hour drive, I was still soaking wet when I arrived in Marianna and decided to stop at my trailer and change my clothes before heading over to relieve Willie at Suzanna's.

It was 3:45 when I turned into my driveway. By 3:55 I was back on the road dressed in dry clothes and with my old service pistol tucked into my belt.

As promised, Willie was parked on the road that leads to Suzanna's, and surprisingly enough he was wide awake.

"Anything?" I asked as I pulled up beside him and rolled down my car window.

"Nada. The house has been dark and quiet since I got here," he answered, the window in his Ford Expedition already down.

"Thanks for helping out," I said, trying to engage him with my eyes so that he could see I really meant it.

"Well, I wish I could say I didn't mind," he said, looking at me steadily.

"This is a bad situation, Willie. I mean—"

He cut me off by holding up his hand and saying, "Don't even want to know. Call me if you get arrested." With that, he cranked his engine and left me in a trail of dust.

I pulled into Suzanna's driveway.

I knocked as hard as I could, thinking it would need to be loud enough to wake her. Within seconds, Suzanna answered the door, dressed in a long nightshirt and a pair of wornout slippers.

"I heard you drive up. Did you get the key?" she asked. It was obvious that she had been awake for a while—if she had been asleep at all.

"Let's sit down," I said, avoiding for a moment, at least, her question.

"Sure. Is everything all right, Hank?" she asked.

"No. Not really," I said as she led us into a room just off the main foyer.

It was a small library with built-in bookshelves covering every inch of wall space and furnished with two end tables, a reading lamp, a leather sofa, and two wing-backed leather chairs. She sat in one of the chairs and directed me to the overstuffed sofa.

"Stan has been murdered," I blurted, more harshly than I really wanted to. The shock that seized her face and body seemed real, but I just watched and waited for her to say something. I wanted to see her reaction. People in these situations often reveal how much, if anything, they know by the questions they ask. She just sat there for a few minutes, her face in her hands, not crying, but visibly shaken.

"That's it? He's been murdered? That's all you can say?" she asked.

"No, there's more. Forgive me. I went up there like you said. The house was dark, and I picked the lock to the side door. When I opened the door, the alarm wasn't on, but I could see the house was a disaster area. As I walked through the house, I could see that someone had systematically searched through the house, looking for something. Everything in every room had been searched. I went into your room, found the key, and was leaving through your husband's room when I saw him ... tied to a chain ... dead." I said.

"Dead?" she asked, looking up from her hands, tears beginning to form in her eyes.

"Dead," I said emphatically, using my eyes to try to deter any further questions about how he died.

So far so good, but her next question sent a shiver down spine.

"Did they get the key?"

I stared at her for a second, not sure how to read her. I was about to answer her question when we both heard a door open in the kitchen.

"Are we alone?" I mouthed the words as we heard at least two, probably more, people entering the house. The confusion on Suzanna's face was unmistakable. I pulled her close to me with one hand and put the other gently over her lips.

"Are we alone?" I whispered into her ear and then looked into her eyes.

Her eyes were wide with fear as she slowly nodded her head.

The footsteps were moving quickly throughout the house, and I knew I had only a matter of seconds to get us out of the house or confront the same fate as Stan.

From the small of my back, I produced the gun which, until this point, Suzanna had not seen. As quietly as possible, I switched the safety off and chambered a bullet.

I grabbed Suzanna's wrist and pulled her with me to the door of the library. I could hear a set of footsteps approaching the library. I positioned Suzanna so that we would be the last things anyone saw if they walked into the room. Someone approached the room carefully, sticking the barrel of a rifle in first. Slowly it moved around the room. I waited until he stuck his face through the door, and I brought the butt of my pistol down on the bridge of his nose with all the force I could muster.

His scream pierced the relative silence of the house, and I could hear all the footsteps begin to converge on the sound. Grabbing Suzanna by the arm, I began to run for the front door, but as I did, I noticed a small bead of red light dancing around on her face. I turned in time to see a man standing at the second-story door with his rifle trained on Suzanna. I squeezed off two shots in his direction as I pulled Suzanna out of his aim and toward the door. By now, the man on the floor at my feet had recovered enough to grab my leg. With a vicious stomp, I brought the heel of my other foot down on his elbow, bending it in a direction I am sure it had never been intended to bend. Again he screamed in pain.

By the time I had finished with him, Suzanna had the front door open, and we made a desperate dash out of the house.

Taking me by the hand, Suzanna led me toward the woods on the north side of her lawn. I noticed another small red light bobbing up and down on her back. I dove and tackled her, just as the whistling sounds of several bullets whizzed overhead and into the trees around us. Rolling onto my back, I raised my gun in the direction of the house and fired three more rounds.

"Ils sont dans l'avant," I heard a man's voice say in French.

I jumped to my feet and pulled Suzanna to her feet. Again I could see four or five of those red lights swirling around. Pulling me by the hand, Suzanna ran toward the closest cover that she could see, while I fired shots back toward the house. Although they had silencers, I could hear the bullets as they thudded into the ground and ricocheted off the trees around us.

"Rapidement, rapidement," a voice from somewhere near the house said.

A few seconds later, we were out of their sights and running through the woods toward the Blue Springs end of the Mill Pond. I could still hear the bullets slashing through the leaves and branches around us as we made our way though woods.

It was a dark night, and twigs and branches were slapping us relentlessly in the face and ripping our clothes. Searching for some kind of a path, I tripped over a log, landing facedown in a mud puddle. Out of breath, I struggled to my feet, checked to see that Suzanna was still with me, and kept running. By then, I could hear them entering the woods and shouting back and forth to one another in words I could not understand.

Suzanna reached back, grabbed my hand, and without a word, changed our course away from the pond. At first I resisted because instead of running away from our pursuers, we began running perpendicular to them. But she insisted. Within a few steps, we were on a trail and again headed away from the men. She dropped my hand and picked up her speed, as I struggled to keep up, fighting for every breath.

Smoothly, Suzanna glided down the path, her steps sure and light. Suddenly, she stopped and looked around and left the trail again. After about a hundred yards, we stepped into a large clearing bordered by a small limestone rock wall. She ran toward the wall, and I followed, tripping twice on loose rocks. Getting up from my second fall, I saw Suzanna half-squatting and trying to wedge herself into a small crack in the wall. She motioned me over and then, as if by magic, disappeared into the rock.

I made my way to the crack as I heard several of the men step off the trail and head toward the clearing. I wasn't as small as Suzanna, and try as I might, I was having little success wedging myself in with her. I could hear the men approaching and was about to abandon the hole and continue running when Suzanna grabbed my hand and with all her might, pulled me into a small limestone cave just big enough for the two of us. It was damp and absolutely dark.

Suzanna leaned over as if to whisper in my ear. I put my finger to her lips, and she complied, sitting back.

The men were at the wall now and sounded as if they were talking on their radio to the others. They carried on a brief conversation and split up to make a thorough search of the area. I could not understand why they couldn't hear my heavy panting. They searched the area for a few minutes, then each took one of the diverging trails out of the clearing.

"Who are they?" was Suzanna's barely audible whisper.

"Don't know," I said even more quietly.

My face and arms stung from the scratches left by the furious sprint through the woods. My back, which could not take much running or sitting in this position, began to hurt.

Nevertheless, we sat quietly until well after dawn.

"We've got to leave sometime," she said, when the morning light shone through a crack so small I was not sure how Suzanna had fit through it, much less me.

"I don't know, I can hole up in here quite a while," I said, unsure what to do next.

"How much longer, then?" she asked.

"If you had seen Stan last night, you would not be in such a hurry to leave, either," I said, regretting it the instant it fell off my tongue.

It took all of two seconds for her to dissolve into tears.

"I'm sorry," I said as I put my arms around her and patted her back.

"What are these people after?" I asked.

"I don't have any idea," she said, fighting hard to maintain her composure.

"Before we worry about any of that, the first thing we've got to do is get out of here," I said, and she acknowledged me with a nod of her head.

I made my way through the small crack that we had used to enter the cave with what seemed like even more effort than it required to get in. I reached back to help Suzanna, who slipped through with quite a bit more ease than I, and I was taken aback by her appearance, but could only assume that I looked the same. Her face was scratched and dirty, her clothes were tattered and torn, and her hair was tangled and matted.

"Oh my heavens, Hank, you look terrible . . . your face . . . do I . . . ?" Her voice trailed off as she looked at her own clothes.

"We need a phone," I said.

"I've got a phone at my house," she said.

"We can't go back there. Those people, they're not going to just forget about you," I said.

"I don't have anything they want," she said.

"We can't go back to your house, and we can't walk through town like this . . ."

"Why don't we just walk up the road and use the Daffins' phone to call the police?" she asked, pointing in the direction the Daffins' house.

"That would be the smart thing to do. But I haven't done the smart thing once since you showed up at my doorstep last week, so I want to make one phone call before we call the police," I said.

We followed a trail up the west side of the Mill Pond, which eventually brought us to the pond headwaters, a swimming hole known as Blue Springs. Blue Springs is Marianna's natural remedy for the dog days of August. One of the largest natural Springs in northwest Florida, a state littered with springs, it pumps out water so cold that it's sure proof the pit of eternal flames could not be located anywhere near Jackson County. In the summer it is quite a popular swimming hole, but with autumn setting in it was closed, and I knew we would find a phone there.

The one call I wanted to make before calling the police was, of course, to Willie. By the time we reached Blue

Springs, it was almost 11:00, and I found Willie in his office.

"Hank, what is going on?" he said when his secretary transferred in the call.

"I wish I knew," I said. "What are you hearing?"

"I'll tell you what I'm hearing. I had two FBI agents in here this morning looking for you and a call from a Sgt. O'Malley of the Atlanta PD looking for you. O'Malley said he knew you."

"Yeah, he's my old captain. What did they want?" I asked.

"Well, they're not looking to update their social calendars," he said incredulously. "I think you know what they want."

"Did you hear what happened out at Suzanna's after you left?"

"What?"

"She had a visit from the same guys who visited her ex. We've been hiding in the woods all night," I said.

"That's all the more reason for both of you to let me come pick you up, and let's talk to these FBI guys. They obviously know something about what's going on," he said, with the rationality that made me call him in the first place.

"Call 'em, and make the arrangements. Then call me at this number," I said, and gave him the number to the pay phone.

"The FBI is already on this thing. We are going to meet with them. Willie is making the call right now," I said to Suzanna after I hung up.

"That was fast," she said, still a little confused.

For the first time, I realized how tired I was. My eyes burned, my head ached, my back was killing me, and my face and arms stung from the dozens of cuts and scrapes we had gotten running blindly through the woods. I stretched out on a picnic table near the phone and waited on Willie's call.

Within a few moments the phone rang.

"Hello," I said, picking it up before the second ring.

"Okay, we're going to do it here in twenty minutes. Can you be here by then?"

"We need a ride—" I was saying, when I noticed four midsize cars make a sharp turn into Blue Springs.

I dropped the receiver and grabbed my gun, which I had left on the table.

"Hank! Hank, you there?" I could hear Willie's voice on the receiver as it dangled from the phone.

Within a matter of seconds, the cars were parked in the parking lot and six of the men waited by their cars, carefully surveying the area, while two more headed in the direction of the snack shack where the pay phone was located.

They hadn't seen me yet. I raised my gun around the corner at the men who were walking toward us.

"That will be close enough," I said, when they were still thirty yards away.

The men on the hill immediately began to scatter and take cover.

"Are you Lafayette Henrie?" the taller man asked.

"I am going to count to ten, and if all six of those men are not on that high-dive platform, one of you guys is dead."

The two men, one considerably shorter than the other, looked at each other, unsure of what they should do.

"One . . . two . . ." I started counting.

"Everybody on that platform, *now!*" yelled the taller man over his shoulder, pointing to the diving platform.

The men I could see just stared at one another.

"Three . . . four . . ." I said, loud enough for them to hear.

"Five . . . six . . ." I cocked my gun and aimed it at the shorter man's head.

"Get on the platform now!" the shorter man yelled, veins bulging on his neck and forehead.

Finally the men started toward the platform, and by the time I reached ten, they were all on their way up to the top. Once they were all on top, I told the shorter man to have the men drop their guns into the spring.

"Throw your guns in the water!" he yelled, barely containing his anger.

"You're making a mistake here, Henrie," said the taller man. "We just want the disk, that's all."

"I'm not talking about anything until they get rid of their guns," I said.

The two men looked at each other. The taller man gave the order.

"Count those guns as they hit the water," I said to Suzanna, without taking my eyes off Shorty. I could tell the men were hesitating, but within a second or two I heard the splashes of the guns as they hit the water.

"That's six," said Suzanna, her voice still shaky.

"Okay, I would like you two gentlemen to lay facedown and spread-eagle," I said, but the men just stared at me.

"Do it *now!*" I said, yelling and startling Suzanna.

Reluctantly, the men got down, first on their knees, and then their stomachs.

"Suzanna, I need you to go and search these men. Can you do that?" I asked, and I took my eyes off the men for the first time since they arrived.

Suzanna was backing slowly away from me, shaking her head.

"Listen to me," I said, alternating my gaze between the men on the ground and Suzanna, "I need you to help me. If one of them so much as twitches, I'll kill 'em."

This did not offer much comfort to her, but I said it more for their benefit than hers. Slowly she started toward them. I talked her through what to do and in moments she had produced a gun, a pair of handcuffs, and a wallet from each of them. I instructed her to cuff each man's hands behind his back. After she had done what I said, I walked over to retrieve the wallets and make sure the handcuffs were tight enough.

I took the wallets and walked back over to the picnic tables, where I could keep an eye on everybody, and opened the wallets.

Both wallets contained badges and FBI identification. One was for Lester Cummings—Shorty—and the other was for Brian Banks.

"I told you you were making a big mistake," said Banks, who was still on his stomach but watching my every move.

"Just shut up," Shorty said.

"What are you doing?" Suzanna whispered. "These guys are here to help us."

"I don't think so. Why would the FBI send these guys out here when we had just made plans to meet them in town? And the FBI doesn't approach people they are trying to help by saying, 'All we want is the disk,' " I explained.

I walked back over to the dangling phone.

"Willie, you there?" I asked.

"Yeah, I'm here. What is going on?"

"I need you to call whoever you set that appointment with at the FBI, and find out why they sent a couple of jerks named Banks and Cummings out here with six of their goons," I said, as Banks and Cummings exchanged glances.

"What are you talking about?" Willie demanded.

"Just what I said. I was on the phone with you and these eight guys showed up with guns and badges claiming to be FBI agents."

"Let me call 'em. Hang on," he said, and put me on hold.

"These guys don't know Banks or Cummings," he said, after a couple of minutes.

"That's what I thought," I said, and hung up before Willie could say another word.

"Okay, 'Cummings,' time for you to come clean. Who are you?" I demanded.

"Look, we just need the disk, that's it. And we got something to trade."

"I don't have a disk and I'm not interested in anything you might have," I said.

"You may not have it, but Mrs. Tanner does. Or you better hope she does, because that disk is your get-out-of-jail-free card," he said.

I looked at Suzanna, but she shrugged her shoulders to indicate that she had no idea what he was talking about. I wasn't sure I believed her, but now was not the time for that discussion.

"What are you talking about?" I asked.

"They've got you, Henrie. They've got you on tape reporting the murder. They've got your fingerprints in the phone booth in Atlanta where the phone call was made. They've got you calling your lawyer less than an hour after the murder. And they got you driving around Atlanta without a license plate less than a hour after the murder," Shorty said.

"That doesn't prove anything," I said.

"Wrong. It goes a long way to proving that you either killed Tanner or you were involved in his murder."

"That's ridiculous. I had nothing to do with it," I said.

"I know that. We know who killed him. I can clear this whole thing up, but we aren't doing anything without that disk, Henrie."

"I don't have your disk, but if I did have it, you can bet you'd pay a higher price than clearing some trumped-up murder charges to get it," I said, and winked at Suzanna, who was standing beside me and holding my arm as if she was about to fall.

"Henrie, I think you got a good look at the handiwork of the people we are trying to keep this disk from. As long as that disk is in the open, whether you know where it is or not, your and Mrs. Tanner's lives are in grave danger.

Does Mrs. Tanner know what happened to her husband?"
asked Shorty.

"Maybe you killed Stan Tanner, and it was you who tried
to kill us last night," I said.

"I am here to help you. Let me up and let's talk," Shorty
said.

"Let me go over what I know for sure with you. You
come down here with six goons from the goon squad, pretending to be FBI agents. You've threatened to have me
arrested for a murder you know I did not commit. You have
just threatened to do to us what you have done to Stan
Tanner. And now I'm supposed to believe that you are here
to help us?"

"Listen, we've gotten off to a bad—"

"Shut up, Cummings. Not another word from you," I
said, as I cocked my gun.

I walked over to where he was lying and rolled him onto
his back. His face and hair were covered in white sand. I
searched his clothes and found his car keys and the key to
his handcuffs. I did likewise with Banks, and I threw everything but one set of keys into the water.

"Let's go," I said to Suzanna.

"Henrie, listen, I'm trying to help you. Help all of us,"
Cummings said. "Inside the breast pocket of my jacket is
a business card. Take it and call me when you have the
disk. We can help each other."

My first inclination was to just leave. But then I realized
that I really did not know what I was involved with. So I
fished around in his pockets until I found the card.

"What are you doing, Hank? These men are trying to
help us," Suzanna said.

"If you would like to stay with these gentlemen, then be
my guest. But I can promise you, they have absolutely zero
interest in helping you. They either killed Stan or could
have saved his life, I don't know which," I said.

"That's not—" Cummings started to say, but using my

gun hand, I delivered a backhand to his jaw that left him limp and unconscious. Then, stepping over Banks, I wedged my pistol into the back of his head and said, "There's plenty more where that came from."

With that, he completely gave in. Suzanna was now in tears, sitting cross-legged on the ground with a blank stare in her eyes and tears running down her cheeks. I walked over and offered her my hand to assist her to her feet. She just stared at me, her eyes glazed with confusion.

"I don't have time for this," I said as I grabbed her by the arm and pulled her to her feet. She offered little resistance as I pushed her toward the cars, keeping a close watch on the diving tower.

I found the car which fit the keys, put Suzanna in the passenger seat, shot the tires out of the other three cars, and left a trail of dust as I headed for the highway. I looked back long enough to see the guys on the platform jump in. I had to laugh because I knew they got the wake-up call of a lifetime.

Chapter Seven

"Don't you even think about looking at me that way," I said to Suzanna, who was sitting as close to her door as she could and looking at me as if I were Hannibal Lecter.

"This time last week, I had a perfect life. I was drawing a check every month. Had a nice place by the river."

She snickered when I said "nice."

"Then you show up out of the blue. And three days later, I got people shooting at me, the FBI thinks I killed your husband, and there's a band of lunatics who want some kind of disk I don't have, but that doesn't matter, because they're willing to kill me whether I've got it or not. And to top it all off, I am driving down the road in a stolen car, my clothes are ripped to shreds, and my face and arms are scratched so badly that it was only slightly preferable to being shot by the men who were chasing us. So, if you have this disk, or know where it is, or have any idea what they're talking about, now would be a good time to share it with me."

"I don't know what they're after," she said.

"These people are after some kind of disk, and it is obvious that they didn't get it from Stan," I said.

"Those last guys, the ones at Blue Springs, they weren't the same as the ones at my house last night. Were they?" she asked.

"It didn't look that way to me. Those guys last night were speaking French. Who knows? But here is what we know. There is a disk somewhere that they want—very badly. They think we've got it. Somebody out there is willing to kill to get the disk. That fun-loving crew we left back there is willing to frame us for murder to get it. And I don't know anything about a disk. That leaves you," I said, gently taking her chin and turning her face so that she had to look me in the eyes. "If there is anything you have not told me about this situation, now would be an excellent time to tell me."

"I don't have any idea what's going on," she said, slapping my hand away from her face and recoiling as far away from me as she could.

"Well, maybe the FBI will know," I said.

"Are you crazy?" she said "Weren't you paying attention to what that guy said back there? They think you killed Stan."

"Those guys back there were not FBI," I said, jerking my thumb over my shoulder in the direction of Blue Springs.

"Maybe they were, maybe they weren't, but those guys were from some government agency. I'd be willing to bet my settlement check on that," she said.

I had to admit that she was probably right; those guys just had the look and feel of G-men.

"Even if that isn't the case, I don't see what good running is going to do. We didn't kill Stan, and we don't have their disk. At least *I* don't," I said.

"Listen, Hank, we are at their mercy if we simply turn ourselves in. Who knows what other mistakes you made while you were in Stan's house. If they can come up with something to prove you were there last night, we're toast. And it won't take them more than two days to find that twenty-five-thousand-dollar cash payment from me to you, either. How's that going to look?" she asked.

"Still, running around in a stolen car is not going to solve any of those problems," I said.

"Don't you see, Hank? We need some leverage. We've got to get that disk," she said with a disturbing clarity.

"How are we going to do that? I can assure you that if it was at Stan's house, they've got it. And you told me that Stan hand-picked the things he sent you after the divorce, so it's a pretty good bet you don't have it, either," I said.

"All true, but there is one thing we know they didn't find at Stan's house. You did get the key, didn't you?"

"Yes," I said, stunned at the clarity of her thinking.

"Don't you see, Hank, that is why Stan took the key—to put something in the box: the disk. That is why he wanted the key back. The disk must be in the safe-deposit box. All we've got to do is go to Grand Cayman and get it."

Chapter Eight

It took me a few minutes to think everything through, but I realized that she might be right. The disk would give us leverage. It wouldn't clear us of the murder, of course, but at least we would have something to negotiate with.

"Our only problem is getting to Grand Cayman," Suzanna said, interrupting my thinking.

"I'm working on it," I said. I was making the plan up as we went along and I had not gotten that far yet. "But before we do anything, we have got to get some clothes and lose this car."

Suzanna was still in her nightshirt and slippers, we were both filthy dirty, and we were driving a stolen car whose owners could not be far behind.

"I don't suppose we could just sneak back into my house?" she asked.

"No, we can't do that. We need some cash from somewhere, and all I've got is a credit card."

"Let's just go by the bank," she suggested.

"We can't go back to Marianna; I'm sure the Feds are all over that place." I was surprised that she had figured out so easily where this disk was, but thought we could just waltz back into Marianna at our leisure.

"It's almost two," I said, looking at my watch. "Here's

55

what we're going to do. We are heading toward Dothan now. Let's keep on going. When we get there, I'll use my credit card to get a cash advance and buy some clothes. We can ditch this car and buy some jalopy for cash. Then do a one-eighty and drive down to Panama City and stay there tonight."

"Why don't we just stay in Dothan?" she asked.

"After we use my credit card, they'll know where we are, if they're paying attention. And I bet they are."

"Well, what are we going to do in Panama?"

"I haven't got that figured out yet."

We took Highway 71 north through Malone, Florida across the state line into Cottonwood, Alabama, on into Dothan. Dothan is a small town of not quite sixty thousand people located in the southeast corner of Alabama less than twenty miles from Florida and Georgia. We hit the circle— a six-lane belt route built around the city in the 1970s— about 2:45. I stopped at the first McDonald's we saw and used what little money I had for a couple of Big Macs and tried to wash up for my trip to the bank. I was able to wash away most of the caked-on mud and dirt, but there was no way to hide the cuts and scratches, or to really clean my clothes.

After eating, we drove to the First National Bank of Do-than. I left Suzanna and her shredded nightshirt in the car.

I approached a teller looking somewhat like a homeless man.

"May I help you, sir?" asked a smartly dressed teller in his early twenties.

"Yes, thank you. I would like to draw five-thousand-dollar advance on my Visa," I said, as I slid the card across a marble-topped counter.

"Certainly, sir," he said, as he looked me over carefully. "I'll need to see some ID with that."

Retrieving my wallet, I showed him my driver's license. He looked at me, then at the license, then at me again.

"Thank you, this should only take a moment," he finally said, before leaving to swipe the card.

As I waited, I noticed at least four video cameras recording the bank's customers and wondered how long it would take before my picture would be on view in some FBI office.

"I'm sorry, Mr. Henrie, Visa is reporting this account closed," the teller said in a slightly nervous voice.

"Excuse me?" I said.

"I swiped the card, and it came back 'account closed.' I'm sorry," he said, as he handed me the card. Then motioning to a blue-haired lady standing behind me, he said, "May I help the next person in line?"

"Hold on a minute," I said, motioning to the lady to wait just one minute. I also carried a credit card that was in my mother's name, but to which I was also a signer-on. I hoped whoever closed my accounts would not have known about this one.

"Let's take it off this card, Mr. . . . Atkin," I said, reading his name tag.

He looked at the card, then at me, then back at the card before saying, "One moment, please." Taking the credit card, he walked out from behind the counter and into an office on the other side of the bank. After five or ten minutes, Atkin came out of the office accompanied by a man in his late forties wearing a tan suit and perfectly coiffed hair.

"How may we help you, Mr. Henrie?" asked the older man, as he approached me with his hand extended.

"You guys have been in that office all this time, and Mr. Atkin here hasn't told you how you can help me?" I asked, shaking his hand.

"Well, yes, he did. He also told me that the first card you tried to use was no good," he said, jerking his head up ever so slightly.

"Yes, there must be some problem that I was not aware

of, but that's no concern of yours. The card you have now should be fine. And I'd like to withdraw the money. I've got a lot to do this afternoon."

"I'll need to see your ID again, son," he said, looking at the credit card and extending a hand toward me.

With an exasperated sigh, I retrieved my ID and handed it to him. He examined them both for a moment and then said, "Mr. Henrie, will you please take a seat over by my office?" he asked, pointing to a leather chair outside his office door. "I'm going to have to make a couple of phone calls."

I almost turned and walked out of the bank. But that card was our only way to get any money, and without any money I might as well turn myself in anyway. So I took the seat as he had requested and waited.

Finally the man stepped out of his office and said, "Mr. Henrie, everything seems okay. I've asked Mr. Atkin to complete this transaction," he said, and turned to walk back into his office.

I followed Atkin back over to the counter to finish the transaction.

Back at the counter, I asked him to give me the money in the largest bills he could. He complied with three one-thousand-dollar bills and twenty-one-hundred-dollar bills.

When he handed me the money, I could not resist holding it up to the camera and giving a wink to whomever it was back at the FBI headquarters who had canceled my cards and would undoubtedly be watching this tape later tonight.

I found an unstrung Suzanna in the car.

"What took so long?" she asked.

"All my credit card accounts have been closed," I said, as I cranked the car.

"Did you get the money?"

"I had to use my mother's credit card, but I got the money. They weren't smart enough to cancel hers yet."

"Who are 'they'?"

"I'm not sure, could be the FBI, could be whoever that was at Blue Springs this morning. Or I guess it could be whoever it was that killed Stan and tried to kill you last night. Whoever it is works very quickly, don't you think?"

"Yes, too quickly," she said, shuddering, as if the news had somehow made her cold.

I pulled into the drive-through of the next bank we came to.

"What are you doing here?" Suzanna asked.

"Just taking a precaution. 'They' may have allowed the bank to give me this money and are planning to track us with the serial numbers. So I want the trail to end here," I said, as I pulled up to the window.

"May I help you, sir?" asked an attractive young lady behind bulletproof glass.

"Yes, can you change these into small denominations?" I asked, placing the three one-thousand-dollar bills in the tray, which she retracted back into the bank.

"Certainly," she said. "Any particular way you would like it?"

"Hundreds and twenties would do fine," I said, putting my car in park.

"I'll be right back," she said, and walked back into the main part of the bank to make sure the bills were authentic, or so I assumed.

Within a minute or two, she was back with a stack of bills that she counted out so I could see them, and we were on our way. I spread the hundreds out over three banks, which took another half-hour. But, satisfied that we had five thousand in untraceable bills, I drove to the Gayfer's parking lot at the Wiregrass Commons Mall.

Suzanna jotted down some sizes on a slip of paper she found in the glove box and I went in and bought a pair of blue jeans and a T-shirt for each of us, and a pair of tennis shoes for Suzanna. I put mine on in a dressing room and returned to the car with Suzanna's.

"Why don't you climb in the back and put these on?" I said. "And then we'll go in and buy another change of clothes each."

She climbed over into the back and began changing. I made a big show of looking the other way as she started to change, but I wouldn't have minded stealing a look. Suzanna kept herself in top physical condition and it showed.

As we were walking in, I gave her a hundred-dollar bill and said, "Find something quick, and meet me at the car in ten minutes."

She looked at the hundred-dollar bill as if I had handed her a gum wrapper and said, "You must be joking."

I handed her another hundred and said, "Whatever you manage to save in there, we can use to keep us alive and out of jail."

Ten minutes later I was back in the car with another pair of jeans, two shirts, and three changes of underwear. I waited for roughly another twenty minutes for Suzanna to return with equivalent clothing from the women's department.

From the mall, we found a little used car lot that only Junior Samples could be proud of on Highway 52 northeast of town.

The salesman greeted us with a big smile and an overly enthusiastic handshake as we got out of the car.

"What can I help you good people with this evenin'?" he asked.

"I need a cheap car that will make it to Atlanta and back without any problems," I said, looking over his underwhelming stock.

"Everything I got's guaranteed trouble-free," he said with a huge grin.

"I'm sure it is, but here's what I'm going to do," I said,

and took two $100 bills out of my front pocket. I tore them in half and handed him half of each bill. "If the car does make the trip without a problem, I'll send you the other halves of those as a bonus."

"How do I know you'll do it?" he said, dropping his I'm-your-new-best-friend shtick.

"These aren't going to do me much good," I said. "Why wouldn't I send them to you? Write your home address on the back of one of your business cards, and I promise you'll get your money—if your car holds up."

Suzanna stood behind me holding my hand. This was a world in which she had no idea how to operate, and she was more than willing to let me do all the negotiations. The salesman was carefully considering each car he had on the lot before walking us over to a 1976 dark brown Chevy Impala.

"This one will make the trip," he said, patting the hood as if it were a prizewinning dog.

I looked it over and started the engine. It was fairly clean and ran well, even though it had 120,000 miles on it.

"How much?" I asked.

"For you? A grand."

"Done," I said, and counted the money out on the hood. Suzanna got our things from the stolen rental car and put them in the backseat, while Ray got us a temporary tag good for one month.

"What should I do with your rental?" Ray asked, as we were driving off.

"Somebody will be around to get it in a day or two. Don't worry," I said, and hit the gas.

We made one more stop for gas and headed for Panama City.

Chapter Nine

Although Suzanna complained about the Chevy, I couldn't tell much of a difference between it and my Jeep as we traveled along Highway 231 toward Panama City.

"Tell me about Stan's business," I said after we had settled into the drive.

"TaraTech? I don't really know that much," she said as she folded her arms over her chest.

"But what does the company do?"

"I don't want to sound like some dumb blond, but I don't really know what they do," she said, looking out the window.

"It's a lot of high-tech manufacturing, isn't it?" I asked.

"They do some manufacturing, but that's not all."

"Like what else?"

"Look, Hank, I barely even know how to turn on a computer. Stan's secretary used to hate me because she couldn't send me e-mail."

"Did Stan do a lot of work in Europe?" I asked.

"Yeah, some. He was over there some," she said, nodding her head.

"Did TaraTech have an office in Paris?" I asked.

"Yes, I believe they did. Why do you ask?"

"I believe the men who broke into your house last night were yelling in French," I said.

"I was so scared, I guess I didn't even notice," she said, looking at her hands, which were now folded in her lap.

"What kind of work did TaraTech do in their Paris office?"

"Hank, I know this is hard to believe," she said, reaching over to squeeze my hand. "And I know it sounds bad, but I really had no idea what he did in Paris. Other than our honeymoon, I was never with him in Paris," she said.

"Eight years of marriage and a no-holds-barred divorce, and you don't know what your husband did for a living?"

"Stan kept his business and his personal life separate. He was obsessive about it. It's not like he was an accountant or something. He was worth hundreds of millions of dollars. His business did a lot of things. And even when things were good between us he kept me out of his business. And to be honest, I never was that interested in it."

"But still you must have some idea," I said, not believing what I was hearing.

"It was very specialized," she said.

"Specialized?" I asked, feeling as though we had made a breakthrough.

"Yeah, Stan would often say that his company was the opposite of Microsoft. They write applications that anybody and everybody can use. TaraTech writes specialized applications to do very specific, highly technical functions. Each customer buys a completely unique product," she said, as though she was reading out of a brochure.

We drove in silence for about forty-five minutes before she said, "You were shot?"

"Excuse me?" I said.

"You said at the truck stop that you were shot in the line of duty," she said.

"Yeah."

"Tell me about it," she said.

I really did not feel like talking about the second incident, so I told her about the first one.

"My partner and I had been working on breaking this car-jacking ring. What these guys would do is spot a car they wanted and follow it home. The next morning they'd be waiting right outside the garage. When the car pulled out of the driveway, they flashed a gun, made the driver stop, and took the car. 'Course, they weren't stealing Geo Metros, they were stealing nice stuff from the nice part of town—you know, Lexus, Mercedes, BMW. Owned by the kind of people who know how to turn the heat up on the department.

"We were spending night and day on it without ever catching a break. I mean we couldn't come up with anything. Nothing. Finally the victims got together and put up a twenty-five-thousand-dollar reward for information leading to the arrest and conviction, blah blah blah.

"Few nights after that, we got our first break. We got a tip about where the next jack was going to be. My partner and I knocked on the people's door about 12:30 A.M. and told 'em what was going on. By the next morning we had the neighborhood pretty well staked out. But the DA had told us we needed to let the jack go down before we made the collar. That way she would have a strong enough case to deal on. Her plan was to offer this guy state's evidence and get him to roll on his buddies.

"So the plan was for me to drive the car out of the garage. When the perp flashed his gun and told me to get of the car, I was to get out and give him the car. We had the car wired on a remote switch so we could turn it off after I got out and then make the arrest.

"Everything went pretty much to plan until it came time for me to get out of the car. As I did my coat got hung up on the seat belt and it opened just far enough for the perp to see my piece. At first I didn't realize what was happening and before I did, Bam, he shot me in the shoulder. Went in here"—I pointed to the part of my arm where vaccinations are usually given—"and came out here." I reached over my shoulder and pointed to a place just past where my shoulder blade ended.

"One of the sharpshooters, stationed on the roof across the street, took him out with a shot to the knee, and it was over."

"How bad was it?"

"Not too bad. Spent two days in the hospital and six months in physical therapy. For years I thought it was worse than it really was. But my shoulder's fine now and I rarely have any problem with it," I said.

"What about the other time?"

"Other time?" I said.

"You got shot," she said.

"Oh, it was nothing," I lied. I just did not feel like getting into that whole thing again.

It was about an hour later when we crossed the Hathaway Bridge, which spans the mouth of the St. Andrews Bay and divides Panama City from Panama City Beach.

Soon after crossing over the bay, we turned south again for a few miles until we reached Highway 98, or what is more commonly known in Panama City Beach as "the Strip."

I had been thinking about a hotel on the beach that would not be suspicious of a couple who wanted to use cash, and decided on the Fountain Bleu, once the crown jewel of the Panama Beach. But that was a long time ago. What's left of its erstwhile glory is now hidden under the grime of neglect. These days, the really nice resorts were found just west of Panama in the beachside community of San Destin.

Suzanna offered little resistance to staying at the Fountain Bleu. After parking the car, I found my way into the lobby and was greeted by a seventy-year-old man with hair dyed jet black and a polyester sports jacket provided by the hotel. He checked me in and didn't even flinch at being offered cash rather than a credit card, although I had to leave an extra fifty dollars as a deposit. Ten minutes later, we were in our rooms and Suzanna was in the shower. When she finally emerged, it was after 7:00. I took a bath as quickly as I could and changed into fresh clothes. I was pleasantly surprised how the scratches on my face looked after a good washing—only a few deeper ones remained visible.

"I'm going to get us something to eat. I'm starving, aren't you?" I asked, after I was dressed and had joined Suzanna in her room.

"I can't decide if I am more tired or hungry," she said from under the blankets of the bed.

"I'll be back in thirty minutes; should I get you something?"

"Yes, but don't wake me if I'm asleep when you get back," she said with a yawn.

I walked out of the hotel and looked up and down the strip. There were two convenience stores an equal distance from the hotel, so I picked one and walked to it.

I bought a quart of milk, a loaf of bread, peanut butter, and some jam. Walking out of the store, I stopped to use a pay phone mounted on the outside wall by the well-used ice freezer. I needed to make a call, and I had been dreading it all day.

"Mr. Free, I have a collect call from Roland Shaffer," said the operator. I had used the name of our second-grade PE teacher. "Will you accept the charges?"

There was a long pause. Too long.

"Mr. Free, are you still there?" the operator finally asked.

"Yes, unfortunately I am. I'll take the call," he said. There was a level of loathing in his voice that I had never heard in the nearly thirty years of our friendship.

"Listen, Willie, I'm sorry. You were right, I was wrong. Not listening to you was the biggest mistake of my life. But all that doesn't change the fact that I'm in trouble and

I need your help," I said as quickly as I could and still sound sincere.

"Have you seen the news, Hank? Have you?" he asked.

"No, I've been driving most of the day," I said.

"You and Suzanna are all over it. You are wanted in connection with Stansfield Tanner's murder," he said.

"You've got to be kidding me," I said, as I set the groceries down at my feet.

"Turn the darn news on if you don't believe me," he said through gritted teeth.

"Please, Willie, I need you to calm down and listen to me. Please?" I pleaded.

"Okay, okay. What?" he asked.

He wasn't exactly calm, but I continued anyway.

"Some guys showed up when I was on the phone with you from Blue Springs. Eight of them. They claimed to be FBI, but when you called the FBI, they didn't know anything about them. Right?"

"Yeah, that's right," he said, the anger beginning to ebb from his voice.

"But they had fake badges, IDs, the works. And the stuff looked real. I've seen some pretty good counterfeit IDs, but I'm telling you, that stuff was good," I said.

"Okay, I got it. They had some good fake IDs."

"Right, they didn't care about anything but some disk. They thought we had it. Said that's what the guys who killed Stan were after, and they would kill us, too."

"I take it you don't have any disk?"

"That's right, but the worst part is, he knew way too much about Stan's murder. He knew I had been there right after the murder, he knew that Atlanta PD had recorded me reporting the murder, he knew I had called you. He knew everything."

"Do they think you killed Stan?" he asked.

"That's the thing, they say they know it wasn't me. They say they even know who did it, but unless I come up with this disk they're going to hang it on me. He said they got evidence tying me to the crime scene. They knew about the money, too."

"What money?" he asked.

"Suzanna gave me twenty-five thousand up front. I deposited it the morning before I drove to Atlanta," I said, embarrassed by my own stupidity.

"What do you mean they're going to hang it on you? You hung it on yourself," he said, back to being angry.

"I know, I know. But I've got to get out of it," I said.

"How're you going to do that?" he asked.

"First thing I'm going to do is get that disk, then I may have something to negotiate with," I said.

"That may or may not be enough for the guys who are trying to kill you. But the real FBI, the ones you stood up in my office today, I don't think they care about a disk. They want you," he said, and I could picture him talking on the phone with no one in the room, but pointing his finger nonetheless.

"Yeah, but maybe I can trade the disk for information on the real killers," I said.

"The 'real killers,' " he said, mocking me.

"Anyway, that's what I'm going to do, unless you can come up with something better," I said.

"What makes you think you can get this disk?" he asked.

"It's a long story, but Suzanna thinks she knows where it is," I said.

"That brings me to another point. How do you know she's not in on this? That she's not the one setting you up?" he asked.

"I can't believe that. For one thing, they broke into her house, just like Stan's—"

"That could have been staged," he interjected.

"Look, Willie, I don't have time to argue with you. Here is what I need from you—" I stopped in mid-sentence when

I noticed two Bay County Sheriff's cars speeding toward the convenience store and slamming on their brakes.

The deputy in the lead car was staring at me through his window. I froze for a split second. I dropped the phone and jumped on a bike that was left in front of the store while its owner was inside.

Before the cars could completely stop, I was around the corner of the store heading for the open fields behind it, pedaling for all I was worth in the direction of a trailer park several hundred yards behind the store.

Within a few moments, the police cars were driving around the store and into the field. It was clear that I could not outrun them. I searched desperately for an avenue of escape, but there was none. I was in the middle of an open field. Just as despair was beginning to set in, the bike fell out from underneath me, and I crashed headfirst into the bank of a small canal running across the field. Before I realized what happened the first car slammed into the bank, barely missing me, but destroying the stolen bike. I scrambled to my feet. The car was nose down in a canal with its rear axle three feet off the ground. The second car hit its brakes, narrowly missing the first.

I had less than fifty yards to the trailer park when the three deputies climbed out of their cars and joined me on foot.

"Bay County Sheriff's office, Henrie. Stop now, or we'll shoot," said one of the deputies.

I glanced back over my shoulder. Two of the men were still chasing me while the third had stopped and was drawing his gun.

I was not less than thirty yards away from a six-foot wooden fence around the trailer park when the first shot pierced the otherwise quiet night. The bullet crashed into the fence in front of me.

"Larry, you're going to kill somebody," yelled one of the officers. I looked back again, and the officer who fired had joined the other two in the foot race. I was putting some distance between me and two of them, but the third was gaining ground on me. I could see that I would have trouble clearing the fence before he caught me. I looked around but had no other choice.

I timed my approach to the fence perfectly, so I could hit it in stride. Leaping with all my might, I grabbed the top with both hands and dove over headfirst, barely releasing the fence in time to break my fall with my hands. As I sprung to my feet, I could hear the faster deputy hitting the fence behind me. Unsure of where to go or what to do, I just ran as fast as I could. The trailers here were parked closer together than trailers normally are. I ran between two of them, tripping on something lying in the grass. Crawling a few steps to get out of sight of the deputy, I began to hear three or four sirens converge on the trailer park. I did not know what to do, but I knew whatever it was, I had to do it fast.

Scrambling to my feet, I glanced back to see what I had tripped over. It was a fiberglass-handled shovel. I picked it up and stepped as close as I could to the nearest trailer and waited for the deputy to make the corner. As he did, I brought the shovel crashing down on the top of his head. His knees buckled under him, and he was out like a light. I quickly ran my hand over his head, where a large bump had already risen—but no blood.

I ran back to the fence. Lying flat on my stomach at its base, I hid in the dark shadows just as the other two deputies were getting around to crawling over. Nervously, I waited, with my heart racing and my chest heaving.

"Where is he, Mark?" one of the deputies yelled, as he swung the beam of his flashlight around the trailer park. I lay only a few feet away in the grass trying to exert some kind of control over my breathing.

Within seconds, the last deputy had made it over the

fence. The sirens were close now, and I could hear the chopping sound of a helicopter approaching.

Lying in the shadows, I waited for the two deputies to move away from the fence. Their diligence in backing up their colleague reminded me of my old partner. Finally their light fell on him. They ran to him, guns pulled, to check that he was all right. Finally a little urgency on their part. I don't know why but it made me feel better. After using their handheld radio to call an ambulance, they separated and started a more diligent search of the trailer park.

The minute they were out of sight I climbed back over the fence and into the open field. The sirens and helicopter were close. Not sure whether I could make it before the other cops arrived, I began to ran back toward the convenience store. Timing my jump, I made it over the canal without tripping. As I neared the store I could hear several sirens as they entered the trailer park and two others as they continued on to the store parking lot. The helicopter was now in plain view as it approached the open field with its powerful searchlight looking for me.

I reached the rear of the store as I heard a sirened car turn into the store's front parking lot. Realizing that there was only one way to drive around the store, I headed for the other side, stepping out of sight as the first of two sheriff's cars drove around the building and into the field. I cautiously made my way to the front of the store. Peeking around the corner, I could see that the way was momentarily clear and I walked with as much control as I could for my bag of groceries, which still sat where I had left them under the pay phone.

Reaching the groceries, I picked them up and walked away from the store as though I were any other customer. As I reached the street I was greeted by another sheriff's car, which was more concerned with getting to the manhunt than with a tourist trying to cross the street. Without so much as a sideways glance he sped past me on his way to the trailer park.

Crossing the street, I allowed myself one backward glance. The helicopter was no more than thirty feet off the ground in the trailer park, searching. I finished crossing the street and walked into the lobby of the Fountain Bleu.

When I got back to the hotel room it was well after midnight. The minute I turned the doorknob, I heard Suzanna begin to stir. When I entered the room I realized she had been up watching the commotion from the window.

"How'd they find you?" she asked.

"Must have had a tap on Willie Free's phone and they traced the call," I said.

"Why were you calling Willie Free?" she asked.

"Because I need his help to get us out of this," I said.

"Why are you calling from a pay phone?"

"Thought it would be safer," I said as I made myself a peanut butter and jelly sandwich.

"Apparently we are all over the news, too. Wanted in connection with Stan's murder," I said, changing the subject a bit.

"Oh, my . . ." she said.

"I know I have asked you about this before, but if there is anything you're not telling me about the mess we're in here, I want to know it now," I said, holding her gaze as long as she would let me.

"What are you saying, Hank? That I killed Stan?" she demanded.

"No, not at all. I'm asking if you know who did it or anything else about it. I need to know. That's all," I said, retreating a little farther than I wanted.

"Hank, don't you think that if I knew something that would help us get out of this situation I would tell you? You think I like to vacation here at the Fountain Bleu? Driving around in a 1976 Chevrolet Impala?"

"Whoa," I said, holding up my hands. "I get it. Sorry I asked."

"What are we going to do? How are we going to get to Grand Cayman? They'll be looking for us at all the airports," she said, moving back to her bed.

"Already thought of that. I used to be friends with a guy by the name of Tommy Carrera. We were on the force together for about six years. Now he owns a seaplane and runs a chartering business out of Mobile. I've always liked Tommy, but I've never been brave enough to fly with him. But now . . . well, it doesn't look like we got a lot of choices."

"That's your plan for getting into Grand Cayman?" she said, more stunned than irritated with the plan.

"You said it yourself—we can't fly. We can't afford to charter a boat. We can't really afford to charter a plane. I'm just hoping I can talk Tommy into doing it for what little we can pay him. We'll probably have to give him some of your jewelry."

"I guess you're right," she said after trying to think of a better plan.

"It's like I once heard, 'Nothing clears the mind like the absence of options,' " I said and took the last bite of my sandwich.

It was well after 1:00 when I finally lay down. It had been over forty-eight hours since I had slept a wink and even though I was bone tired I did not sleep very well. When the 6:30 wakeup call came, and Suzanna knocked on my door, my back and knees hurt so badly I felt incapable of getting out of bed. Gradually, with every joint in my body creaking and popping, I forced myself.

"Gee, Hank, no wonder they put you on disability," Suzanna said, as she watched me make my way to the bathroom.

I turned the shower on as hot as I could stand it and let

the heat begin to loosen my back muscles. Slowly they began to respond, starting with my lower back, then moving gradually up my spine, spreading to my shoulders, and up my neck, finally, to the base of my cranium. But I knew the pain would not leave completely until I went to see my physical therapist. I had missed one of my three regular weekly appointments on Monday, and today I would miss a second. That was not good.

When the heat and water had done all it could, I toweled off and got dressed. Forty-five minutes later, we were headed east on Highway 98. I halfway expected a roadblock somewhere, but we drove unmolested out of Panama City and toward Pensacola.

We stopped in Fort Walton for gas and we each bought a pair of sunglasses and a baseball cap to serve as a disguise. With that, twenty gallons of gas, two stale cinnamon rolls, and a quart of orange juice, we were on our way again.

We followed Highway 98 along the northwest coast of Florida until we reached Pensacola, where we stopped at a pay phone. It took longer than expected to find a phone number for Tommy Carrera in Mobile, Alabama. I called Tommy and told him I was coming over and had a job for him. He gave me directions to his place, and we were on the road again, taking I-10 into Mobile, then I-165 into Chickasaw, a small suburb of Mobile.

After making a few wrong turns, I finally found Tommy's house on a dead-end street. It was a smallish rambler, which had not been very well kept up. As Suzanna and I made our way up the small cement walkway leading to the front door, I realized that my back had reached its capacity and would completely go out unless I gave it some rest. I was unable to stand up straight or move without severe pain.

When we reached the door, I leaned my arm and head against a wooden post supporting the roof of the house's small porch. Suzanna, sensing that I was in real pain, grabbed my arm as if trying to hold me up and knocked on the door.

A young blond wearing a bathing suit and a pair of blue jean cut-off shorts answered the door.

"You must be Mr. Henrie," she said to me, as she opened the door. "Y'all come on in."

"Tommy didn't tell me he had a daughter," I said through gritted teeth.

"I'm not his daughter, silly. I'm his girlfriend," she said with a smile you might expect from a Best-In-Show dog owner.

Although this caught me by surprise, Suzanna was unfazed, and she politely extended her hand to the girl.

"I'm Suzanna Tanner, a friend of Mr. Henrie's."

"Nice to met y'all. I am Jasmine Summer," the girl said as she and Suzanna exchanged an awkward handshake.

"Please call me Suzanna."

"And I'm Hank," I said as I made a vain attempt to stand up straight and was acutely aware of how old I must look.

"Tommy's at the grocery store. He said for me to make you feel at home," she said.

"I just need a hard surface to lie on, before my back completely gives out on me," I said.

"What's wrong, Mr.—I mean, Hank?" she asked, as she grabbed my arm and helped me to the floor in a small sitting room just off the main hallway. The carpet was old and matted but looked clean. But my back was hurting so badly at that moment, I would have lay on the floor of a public bathroom and been glad to do it.

"Nothing my physical therapist couldn't fix," I said, as I made my way to the floor. Suzanna asked to use the bathroom, and Jasmine gave her a brief set of directions as I attempted to get comfortable.

"I'm not a physical therapist," Jasmine explained, "but I

did go to massage therapy school for almost a year. Want me to give you a massage?"

I felt a little awkward, but my back was killing me, and I had to have some relief.

"Well, if it isn't too much trouble," I said.

"Don't be silly. Tommy says I give the absolute best backrubs," she said.

"That would be nice," I said.

"Take your shirt off and roll over on to your stomach. I'll get my massage oil," she said as she left to room.

She was back momentarily with a bottle of oil, and I was lying on my stomach.

"All ready?" she asked.

"I guess so."

She went to work without another word. Starting at the small of my back, she began to massage. The oil was warm, and her hands were soft and firm as they worked against the tenseness of my muscles. Gradually they relaxed, as she worked with a slow easy rhythm, gradually working her way up my back, massaging me in exactly the right way—almost as if she were reading my mind. Like the tide going out at dusk, slowly, almost imperceptibly, the pain flowed out of my body. As it left, I began to realize how tired I was. I had slept only five of the last sixty hours. I was aware that at some point Suzanna came into the room and spoke with Jasmine, but other than that I was unaware of my surroundings, slipping deeper and deeper into a slumber and aware only of the soothing rhythm of Jasmine's massage.

Chapter Ten

When I emerged from my nap it was dark outside and I lay on the floor, still shirtless but with a blanket covering me and a pillow under my head. At first I didn't realize where I was, but as I lay still, my mind gradually began to clear.

"You awake?"

It was the voice of Tommy Carrera, sitting on a chair in front of me.

"Yeah, what time is it," I asked, cautiously moving my back to see how it would react.

"It's about seven-thirty. So you killed Stan Tanner?" he asked with a mischievous smile.

"Where'd you hear that?"

"It's all over the news that he was murdered day before yesterday, and you and his old lady are wanted for questioning," he said in a tone that almost suggested that he was envious of my situation. Tommy is tall and lean with long, curly blond hair that is forever hanging in his face. His eyes, which used to be a clear blue when we were on the Atlanta PD together, were now gray and clouded, but the same happy-go-lucky attitude he had back then was still evident in each footstep and in his ready smile.

"To answer your question, no, I didn't kill him, but I'm being set up for it," I said, aware of how lame it sounded.

"Set up," Tommy said mockingly, before taking a long swig off a beer I had not noticed.

"I know it sounds bad, but let me explain," I said as I made my way up to a standing position.

"That Jasmine is a miracle worker," I said. "When I came in here my back hurt as bad as it has since I was in the hospital. Now it feels better than it ever has since the accident."

"Good, let's go for a walk," he said and also stood up.

"What about Jasmine and Suzanna?"

"They went out to get some dinner."

"You think that's smart?" I asked.

"They'll be fine. They're just picking up some takeout from a Chinese place up the road," he said as he held open the front door.

It was a cool, breezy evening and as we stepped onto the sidewalk in front of Tommy's house, I noticed that the moon was full and bright, making the streetlights that dotted the street seem unnecessary. I stopped by our car, which was parked on the curb, and retrieved the hat I had bought at the gas station in Fort Walton. I adjusted the hat and put it on.

"Okay, tell me what's going on," Tommy said, and he indicated the direction he wanted to walk.

I was going to need Tommy's help, so I thought it would be best just to tell him everything. So I started with Suzanna's first visit to my trailer and told him everything that had happened right up to pulling up into his driveway. As I did Tommy walked with his hands in his pockets, staring at the ground in front of his feet, concentrating on what I was saying.

"So what is your plan?" he asked, still not looking up.

"I need to get to Grand Cayman and get that disk," I said.

"And you want me to fly you down there," he said.

"I've got about three thousand dollars in cash, and Suzanna says there is several hundred thousand dollars in jewelry in the box. If you are willing to take the risk, I think I can make it worth your while."

"If these Frenchmen and those other guys—whoever they are—are after the key, they probably know about the safe-deposit box, and if they do, you can bet they got people watching it twenty-four/seven."

"That's true, but if you're willing to help me, I think I've got a plan."

"I think the price tag for this little trip just went up," Tommy said, looking at me for the first time since I started my story.

"These Frenchmen think we have the key and are expecting me or Suzanna to show up to get the disk from the box, right?" I asked.

"Yeah, but what about the FBI and these other guys who showed up at that Blue Springs place. Do they know about the key?"

"I'm not sure, but I don't think so. If they do, they didn't mention it."

"Okay, I'm with you, go ahead."

"Here's what we'll do. You go into this bank and open a new safe-deposit box. While you're in there, you can scout the place out. If it's like these banks normally are, they will take you to your box and use their key to open their side of the lock while you use yours to open your side. Then you take the entire box into a small private room where you can remove or add whatever you like."

"Okay, I'll open a box, then we'll have two," he said.

"Right. The next day, I'll come in and ask to open Suzanna's box. Once I have the box and I'm in one of those private rooms, you'll come in and ask to get into your box. I'll wait for you in the private room. Then I'll give you the disk and jewelry and you leave. Once you've had time to get far enough away, I'll leave. If I have been spotted, that's when they will move. But it will be too late; you'll be gone with the disk and the jewelry."

"There is only one problem with that plan."

"That is?"

"They killed Stan when he couldn't produce the key. What makes you think they won't kill you when you can't?"

"This is where the plan gets a little risky. I hope to get in and out of there without being noticed. But just in case, I'm going to take a disk down there with me and when confronted trade it for my freedom."

"Yeah, I'd say that's a little risky. Suppose they are not in a mood to trade. Maybe they'll just kill you and take the disk," he said flatly.

"Well, I have certain advantages that Stan didn't have," I said.

"Such as?"

"They will not have the element of surprise on me. Hopefully, I can avoid even being caught by these guys. That's number one. Number two is, I'll be giving them what they want, at the very least, and it will take some time to realize that it is a fake. That should buy me some time. And number three, I know how to handle myself better than Stan," I said, with all the confidence I could muster.

"I don't know if I would want my life resting on those advantages, but that's your call. The way I see it, I'll be long gone before any of that stuff goes down," he said.

"That's the way I see it, too," I said.

It was 8:30 when we turned and headed back for Tommy's house. My back still felt great. We walked into a small strip mall so I could use a pay phone to call Willie. It was Wednesday night, and on Wednesday nights Willie was always at choir practice. And I was pretty sure that the FBI would not have bugged the phone at Poplar Hill Baptist Church. At least not yet.

I called information for the number and dialed the church. It must have rung ten or eleven times before someone answered it.

"Hello," said the voice of a young girl.

"Hello. Is Willie Free there?" I asked.

"Yeah. But he's singing," she said.

"Would you please tell him he has an urgent phone call? I think he will want to take it," I said in my kindest and sweetest voice.

"Well, they usually don't like me to bother 'em when they're practicing," she said, and I could hear the choir begin a new song in the background.

"Can you please make an exception just this once? I know Mr. Free will want to talk to me."

"Well, okay, I hope you are not going to get me in trouble," she said.

"I'm sure you won't, sweetheart," I said as she plunked the phone down on something hard.

A minute or two passed before Willie picked up the phone.

"Hello," he said.

"It's me," I said.

"I was hoping you'd call me here tonight," he said. "Hang on while I close the door." There was a pause as I heard a door shut.

"Okay, I'm back. Listen, I've got some information for you. You all right?" he asked as I heard the noise an office chair makes as it leans back. I could picture Willie kicked back with his feet on the preacher's desk.

"I'm fine. You know they got your phone bugged," I said.

"I figured. I heard what happened in Panama City last night. It was on the news this morning."

"Yeah, I'll explain it all later. What do you have for me?"

"First of all, whoever those men were at Blue Springs

yesterday, they weren't FBI. They never heard of any Cummings or Banks," he said emphatically.

"Who were they then?"

"FBI doesn't know," he said.

"How do you know that?"

"That is what I'm trying to get to. You got a minute?"

"Yeah, go ahead," I said, motioning to Tommy that this was going to take a while. He shrugged his shoulders and walked into a frozen yogurt place two doors down from the phone.

"Back in my college days, I played football with a guy who is now an FBI agent. Started as a special agent, but has worked his way up now pretty high in the Bureau. By the way, this has got to stay between you and me. What I'm about to tell you, he had no business telling me, and if it gets out that he did, they'll nail him for obstruction of justice."

"It's all dead-man talk with me," I said.

"Good. First a little background. You ever hear of a guy named Philip Zimmerman?

"I don't think so."

"Neither had I until this morning. Back in the early 1990s, he wrote an e-mail software program called Pretty Good Privacy, PGP for short. Anyway, its basic function was to encrypt ordinary e-mail messages so that they could travel securely over the Internet. How much do you know about encryption?" Willie said.

"Not much."

"You need to get out of your trailer more. I don't want to get too technical here, but essentially, encryption is the use of algorithms to encode and decode messages. What they do is turn text or data into kind of a digital gibberish, and then when the info is needed they use a key to restore it to its original form. Okay. The longer the key is, the harder the code is to break.

"To decipher an encrypted message without the key, you

would have to use every possible key until you found the right one. These keys are made of what they call bits. An eight-bit key has 256 possible solutions. A 56-bit key, which is considered small by today's standards, has 72 quadrillion possible combinations. If the key is 128 bits long, roughly the equivalent of a sixteen-character message on a personal computer, it would have 4.7 sextillion possible combinations. That's a 4 and a 7 followed by twenty zeros. Got all that?"

"Well, considering I can't keep my checkbook balanced, I think I'm doing all right," I said.

"With your average PC, you can crack a 56-bit key. But a 128-bit key is considered unbreakable. Until a couple of years ago, the U.S. government considered anything longer than a 40-bit encryption to be munitions, just like guns or warheads or anything like that, and it was illegal to export."

"E-mail software is a weapon?" I said, unsure I had heard him correctly.

"Yeah, it's classified that way, anyway. The problem is that the government believes this stuff is going to severely limit its ability to spy on our enemies or keep an eye on what terrorist groups are up to. So they are trying to control it."

"I see," I said.

"Back to Philip Zimmerman and his e-mail software. When his little program started showing up in other countries, the Justice Department and the FBI launched a three-year investigation. They never did charge him with anything, but the battle between the government and the techies was on. The Justice Department had lost the first round; they weren't going to lose the second.

"Enter TaraTech, Stansfield Tanner's company, a leading developer of high-end encryption software. Stan had the latest and greatest, but the federal government was severely limiting his market. According to my buddy, sometime early last year, Stan was approached on a business trip to

Paris by agents from French Intelligence, who wanted his company's help in developing an encryption program. I don't know how the FBI found out about it, but they did. And they were going to make Stan the poster boy for why the government needed to control this stuff.

"So they started this investigation, and it went on for over a year. Stan was pretty good at covering his tracks, but apparently the FBI had someone on the inside. They were getting close to finishing the deal about six months ago when something went wrong and Stan completely cut off all communications with his contacts. The FBI and Justice Department were not sure what to do. Their conspiracy case was weak. As near as they could tell, Stan was never paid and no technology was ever transfered. Apparently they had just decided to seat a grand jury and try the conspiracy case when Stan was murdered."

"So they know who killed Stan," I said, "Why are they trying to hang it on me?"

"That's the problem, Hank, they don't know. They suspect French Intelligence and you. As far as the French go, the Feds have very little evidence that points to them, and they got a lot that points to you. My guy's telling me they don't know who it was for sure."

"What do you have on me?"

"More than enough to get an indictment. First the obvious stuff, the police report and the driving without a license plate. They got a recording of you reporting the murder to the Atlanta PD over a pay phone less than a half-mile from Stan's house. They got the phone records of a call from another pay phone near my house. They got witnesses putting you and Suzanna together at the truck stop and at Grady's. They got her withdrawing twenty-five thousand in cash last week and you depositing that much on Monday. They found a used pair of latex gloves in the car you rented and left at Suzanna's. And finally, they've got carpet fiber in the rental car that matches the carpet in Stan's house."

After he finished, there was a dead silence. I could not speak. It was as if a noose had been tightened around my neck, preventing even a breath from escaping my lips. My mind was reeling, unable to focus.

"That's all circumstantial," I finally said, when the silence had become too awkward to stand.

"Yeah, but people get convicted every day on less evidence than that," Willie said, unwilling to let me have any comfort.

"What about Suzanna's house? They trashed it, too," I said.

"Their theory is that you and Suzanna could have just been trying to cover your tracks."

As we walked back to his house, I tried to make small talk with Tommy to catch up with what had happened to him since I'd last seen him. He had kicked around from one job to another before opening his chartered plane business, and that had been going pretty well. His first two wives had left him, each divorce sending him into a downward spiral that ended in a detox center. He had met Jasmine—who really was older than she seemed—on one of his charter flights, and they had been involved for about four months. Tommy had a lot to say, but I could concentrate on none of it. All I could think about was how important it was to get that disk and how much the success of my plan depended on a guy whose whole life is comprised of a series of episodes which began with the best intentions but inevitably ended up with him disappointing the people who were counting on him the most.

When we got back to Tommy's house, it was well after 10:00. Jasmine was asleep in the only bedroom, and Suzanna had curled up with a blanket and a pillow on the couch in the family room. They had left a couple of cold egg rolls, sweet-and-sour pork, and ham fried rice on the kitchen table. Tommy and I finished off the food before turning in for the night, Tommy to the bedroom and me to the floor in the family room.

The room was perfectly still and dark except for the moonlight streaming in through the front window. Although I was tired, I could not help but think about my conversation with Willie. It had taken the FBI less than forty-eight hours to build a convincing case against Suzanna and me. But none of the evidence—all of which pointed to my guilt—was fabricated. It was all real. Yet, I could not figure how I came to be a suspect so quickly. It wasn't that they knew about me and my activities on the night of Stan's murder that surprised me, it was how quickly I became a suspect. One minute the FBI is building an espionage case against Stan, the next I am their prime suspect in his murder. There had to be more going on than I knew about.

Then there was the problem of Banks and Cummings—who were they really? They certainly looked, talked, and acted like government agents. How did they fit into this problem? If they were working for the French, how did they know about the disk? Maybe they did work for French Intelligence. Maybe they didn't.

Also there was the problem of the disk. It was the key to my freedom. But for a key to be any good, it needs a lock. So what if I got the disk. That would not prove to the FBI that Suzanna and I did not conspire to kill Stan. All it would likely prove is that Stan was, in fact, involved with the French in something that was illegal. So giving the disk to the FBI did not necessarily get Suzanna and me off the hook.

That brought me back to Banks and Cummings. They had said they had proof about who killed Stan that they would trade for the disk. It looked as though I was going to need the business card I had taken out of his pocket after all, leaving me to hope that they could actually make good on their word to prove who Stan's killers really were. I desperately wanted to go to sleep, because the more I thought about the predicament my foolishness and greed had gotten me into, the more physically ill I became. The twenty-five thousand sitting in my bank account now seemed more like a millstone around my neck than the nest egg I thought it would be.

As I lay in the dark trying to force sleep to come, Suzanna whispered, "You awake?"

"Yeah, I thought you were asleep," I whispered back.

"Off and on. This couch is not the most comfortable."

"The floor's not much better."

"You and Tommy get a plan worked out?"

"Yeah, we're leaving in the morning, be back the day after."

"You're not leaving me here, are you?" she said, propping herself up on her elbow.

"I think it's best."

"Why?"

"Well, the authorities are expecting us to be together. I'll be less noticeable without you. And we don't really need you to get the disk. A third person would just be in the way."

"So what do you want me to do while you're gone?" she asked, laying her head back onto her pillow.

"Best thing for you to do is stay right here, inside the house, and don't make any phone calls. Chances are, everybody you know has their phone tapped."

"I'd rather go with you."

"Yeah, I know. But this is the best way," I said through a yawn. A minute later we were both asleep.

Chapter Eleven

T he next morning Tommy woke me up just after dawn
with a nudge from his foot.

"Need to get going. Got a lot to do," he said as he bent
over to offer me a piece of dry toast and black coffee.

I was anxious to get going as well, so I drank the coffee
black—which I never do—and ate the toast in three bites.
After taking a quick shower, I left a note for Suzanna, who
was still asleep on the couch:

Suzanna,
    Sorry we had to leave before you woke up. I wanted
to tell you about a conversation I had with Willie Free
last night. But I guess it will have to wait until I get
back. If something happens, contact Willie. He knows
what's going on and will be as much help as anyone
could be. Please stay inside and don't call anyone until
I get back. See you tomorrow.

Hank

Two hours later Tommy and I were in his seaplane on
Mobile Bay preparing for take off. While Tommy readied
the plane and filed his flight plan, I had taken his truck
back into town. Where, after considerable effort, I found

an open computer store not far from the University of South Alabama Medical Center and bought a blank CD-ROM to use as a decoy. Then, after finding an open discount store, I bought a couple of gym bags for Tommy and me to use in the exchange.

Tommy's plane was bright orange and looked as though it might be a World War II relic. He advertised the plane as large enough to seat eight, and there are eight seats, but I could not see how more than three people could be comfortably accommodated.

The trade winds were stiffer than normal causing the water of Mobile Bay to white cap. Even though I was used to being on small boats, staring out the front window of the plane through the spinning propeller as the horizon bobbed to and fro was making me seasick. Tommy, unaware of my churning stomach, was studiously checking his gauges and making notes on a clipboard. No matter how sick I was feeling, I was not about to interrupt that.

"You ever been in a seaplane before?" Tommy yelled over the roar of the engine when he was finally ready for takeoff.

"No. This is my first time," I said.

My palms were sweaty, my mouth dry as he throttled up the engine and made the bumpy ride up to flight speed. After we had taxied for what seemed like too long, we lifted off and were on our way to Grand Cayman.

Tommy pointed out a few landmarks as he flew, but for the most part we made the four-and-one-half-hour flight without conversation. Despite my fears, the landing in Spanish Bay off the coast of Grand Cayman was as uneventful as our takeoff. We taxied into Morgan's Harbour on the northwest tip of Grand Cayman and docked the plane.

"What now?" Tommy asked when we were both standing on the dock.

"I don't think it's good for us to be seen together," I said.

"Agreed," said Tommy a little too anxiously.

"Why don't you jump in a cab down to Ambassador Inn just off Seven Mile Beach and check in? After you're in the room I'll call and get the number and meet you there," I said.

"Sounds like a plan. Ambassador Inn just off Seven Mile Beach?" he said, confirming his instructions.

"That's right, the cab driver will know where it is," I said.

After finding a cab he was on his way.

With Tommy gone I ventured over on foot to the little town of Hell. Situated on rocky Ironshore Beach not far from Morgan's Harbour, Hell features a post office from which tourists send letters and postcards to friends all over the world postmarked Hell. Browsing around the little town, I noticed many of the locals and tourists were decked out in pirate garb. I stopped a friendly-looking local with a half-empty bottle of rum in his hand and asked about the costumes.

"Pirate's Week. You are now in pirate country and this is the week we celebrate our swashbuckling heritage," he said in a cadence that suggested he had memorized the line from some tourism brochure.

"You dress like this all week, then?" I said.

"And drink rum. The costume is optional; the rum is not," he said with a smile, and took another long draw on his bottle.

"Tomorrow, too?"

"Oh, yes, tomorrow's the big day. We kidnap the governor, you know," he said as though he were the key member of a conspiracy.

"Kidnap the governor?" I said, wondering if the rum was talking.

"It's part of the tradition. We do it every year," he said as he grabbed my arm to keep himself from falling over.

"I see. That does sound like fun," I said as I helped him back on his way.

Finding a pay phone, I called the Ambassador Inn and asked for Tommy's room. He answered on the third ring and gave me the room number. I found a cab and asked the driver to take me to the Ambassador Inn. The pirate costumes, I thought, might be the extra twist my plan needed. Without a doubt the bank would be watched twenty-four hours a day. And by now these people would know that I was involved with Suzanna and would be looking for me as well as her. A pirate's costume might be just the thing I needed to get in and out of the bank without being noticed and at the same time not raise the suspicions of the bank's staff.

The Cayman Islands are a mecca for scuba divers and when scuba divers on a budget come to Grand Cayman the Ambassador Inn is the place they stay. It's about a mile north of George Town, the islands' capital and two hundred yards inland and across West Bay Road. It's not the nicest place to stay, but it did have the three things which were required most for this visit to Grand Cayman—cheap rates, private baths, and air-conditioning.

By the time I got to the room it was well after 3:00 in the afternoon and we were running out of time for Tommy to get the new safe-deposit box opened. The room was small but clean with two double beds. Tommy had already picked the one closest to the door and reserved it with his overnight bag. I dropped my bag on the bed by the window.

All the positive benefits from Jasmine's massage were now a distant memory and I needed to rest my back. Making a considerable effort to get onto the floor, I tried to find a comfortable position to lie in while Tommy and I went over the plan for the afternoon again.

"The most important thing to remember is to make sure

no one—I mean *no one*—follows you back here. You do remember how to shake a tail feather, don't you?" I asked after we had gone over the plan one more time.

"Yeah, man, I got it all down," he said.

"Now when you get back, I won't be here," I said. I wanted to go out and buy a pirate costume while he was gone and then watch as he returned to make sure he wasn't followed.

"Want something for your back?" he asked.

"I need either my pills, my physical therapist, or Jasmine. Nothing else helps," I said.

"What kind of pills?" he asked, pulling a shaving kit from his overnight bag.

"I've got some muscle relaxers that my doctor prescribes," I said.

"What are they?" he said as he rummaged through what sounded like dozens of half-empty pill bottles.

"Carisoprodol," I said.

"That's pretty tame stuff," he said as he tossed me a half-empty prescription with the name of Richard McDaniel on it.

"Where'd you get this stuff?" I asked. But then I held up my hand to stop him from answering. "Never mind, I don't want to know. Just get me a glass of water."

He brought me a glass that was too full to drink from while lying on my back. With difficulty I sat up far enough to take the pills.

"You gonna be all right, then?" he said after I was horizontal again.

"Yeah, see you back here in a couple of hours," I said.

I lay on the floor for another fifteen minutes after Tommy was gone, waiting for the muscle relaxers to kick in. Gradually my back started to loosen up and I started getting sleepy—an inevitable side effect of the medication.

Getting off the floor, I changed into a T-shirt and a pair

of shorts and headed out of the hotel. I stopped at the front
desk and conferred with the manager about Pirate Week.
He confirmed everything my rum-drunk friend from the
town of Hell had told me a few hours before. I asked him
where to get a good pirate's costume and he directed me
to a shop in George Town which catered to tourists. I
hopped a cab into town, found the shop, and bought a big
blousy shirt, a wide-brimmed hat with one side pinned up,
a large white feather, and the obligatory eye patch.

With the costume in hand, I found a dive shop and rented
a pair of binoculars and caught a cab back to the Ambassador Inn. Instead of going in, I perched myself across West
Bay Road on Seven Mile Beach so I could watch the com-
ings and goings at the Inn. It was a warm day with a few
high clouds, and the beach was full of scuba divers slapping
one another's backs, exchanging tales of the day's adven-
tures. I enjoyed eavesdropping on their conversations as I
watched the Ambassador for Tommy's return.

I waited for about thirty minutes before Tommy showed
up and nonchalantly walked in the front door. I continued
to watch for about another thirty minutes and saw nothing
out of the ordinary before deciding it was safe to join him
inside.

When I walked into the room Tommy was lying on the
bed with his shirt off, watching the TV.

"How did it go?" I asked as I sat down on the bed next
to his.

"Without a hitch," he said as he dug a key out of his
pocket identical to Suzanna's.

"I guess we're in business, then," I said. "Tell me about
the bank."

For the next hour I quizzed Tommy on everything that
had happened while he was at the bank. How many people
worked at the bank? How did the people act? How was the
floor plan laid out? I was pleasantly surprised at the amount
of information Tommy remembered and how well it

aligned with Suzanna's description of the bank. Even though I had never been in the bank or even seen a diagram of its floor plan, I felt like I knew the bank as well as any building I had been in.

After I was satisfied that I had learned everything about the bank that Tommy knew, we began going over our plan for getting the disk out. Undoubtedly there would be people watching the bank. These people would be looking for either Suzanna or me. The trick to this plan would be to get Tommy in and out of the bank without raising suspicions. We had to be in and out as quickly as possible and Tommy had to look like any other bank patron conducting his business.

As we were going over the plan, Tommy began to get nervous and threatened to back out. I had to reassure him that whatever jewelry was in the box would be his if he would only see this thing through. Dangling money in front of Tommy worked as well on him as it had on me and I felt reasonably sure that I could count on him to at least show up at the bank. What would happen after he left the bank with the jewelry and the disk I was less sure about. But I had known all along that the plan was flawed in two critical areas, and Tommy's reliability was one of the biggest flaws.

It was well after dark when we finished going over our plans for the next day and the muscle relaxer was beginning to wear off. I sent Tommy out to pick up some dinner and I took a hot bath to loosen my back muscles. He was back in about an hour with burgers, fries, and drinks from the Hogs Sty Bay Café in George Town.

I had not eaten anything since the coffee and toast Tommy had served me for breakfast, so I swallowed mine just about whole and took another one of Tommy's pills with my last swallow of Coke.

*   *   *

I awoke the next morning from a restless sleep with a softball-size knot in my stomach. I had tossed and turned the whole night thinking about our plan. Tommy was unreliable, yet I hoped that the lure of the jewels would at least get him to the bank. But in reality, I couldn't even be sure of that. Assuming he came to the bank, I was increasingly concerned that he would not even wait long enough for me to elude whatever problems I had leaving the bank. But, I told myself, even if he did try to take the money and run, he would be easy to track down. Although enough to sink my plan, the concerns about Tommy were the least of my worries. My major concern was that I had very little idea what I would be facing as I left the bank. Whoever these people were they would not move on me until I had the disk, so I knew I was safe on my trip to the bank. I would have much to worry about while in the bank since banks like these are considered sacrosanct. Leaving the bank was the biggest vulnerability in the plan. I knew these people, whoever they were, were merciless—the recurring memory of Stan Tanner's body was all the proof I needed of that. I didn't know from where they would be watching, how many there were, or how they would attack. The only thing I knew for sure was if I were spotted, they would attack. Since I didn't know how or when the attack would come, I had no way to prepare for it. The only thing I could do was be alert as I left the bank and get off the island as soon as possible.

If I were caught I had the decoy disk, which would only fool them for a while, but provide time for an escape attempt. Thinking of my plan only made the knot in my stomach grow larger. But I also realized that the plan I had devised was my best shot.

I took a quick shower and volunteered to go out for breakfast while Tommy was getting ready. Finding a convenience store close to the Inn was not hard. I picked up some powdered doughnuts and two hot coffees. Back at the room I found Tommy ready and waiting. We each ate a couple of doughnuts and drank the coffee. I put my pirate costume over my clothes. As we finished eating, I went over the plan one more time with Tommy and said, "Remember, when you leave the bank, come straight back to this hotel room and wait for me to call. I won't come here for any reason, so don't answer the door if anybody knocks. Got it?" I said, trying to look him in the eye.

"Got it," he said.

"If I don't call you by morning, call Willie Free at this number. Let him know what has happened and leave without me," I said, jotting Willie's number down on a small pad of paper provided by the Inn.

"Didn't you say his number has a wire on it?" Tommy asked.

"If I'm not back by morning, it won't matter who's listening. I'll see you in the bank," I said.

Before leaving I checked the zippered pocket of my bag one more time for the decoy disk. Finding it there, I left for the bank.

Chapter Twelve

It was a warm, breezy day under a cloudless sky as I stepped out of the cab in front of CayBank. The weather, however, was the furthermost thing from my mind. My breath was short and a feeling of claustrophobia I had not felt since childhood began to creep into my mind.

CayBank is officed in a white-and-blue, three-story building which looked as though it had been remodeled from a large nineteenth-century plantation house. About fifteen yards from the curb there are two small patches of grass on either side of a cement walk connecting the curb with the front door of the bank. On the left side of the building is a driveway which leads from the street in front to a parking lot in the rear of the building.

Trying to look as casual as possible, I surveyed the surroundings but could see nothing out of the ordinary. In the distance, in the center of George Town, was the Clock Tower, which, although it was only a few blocks distant, seemed miles and miles away.

Taking a deep breath, I walked purposefully to the front door and entered the bank. A beautiful, dark-haired woman sitting behind a tall mahogany receptionist's desk greeted me. Tastefully mounted on the wall behind her desk in elegant brass letters was the word *CayBank*. Self-conscious about wearing a pirate costume, I was relieved that the receptionist was not at all surprised to see a man dressed like Captain Hook standing in her lobby. Nevertheless, I could not resist the urge to take off the hat and eye patch and put them in my bag.

"May I help you, sir?" she said in unaccented English and with a warm smile.

"Yes, I need to get into my safe-deposit box," I said as I produced the key from my pocket as proof that I did indeed have a box.

"Of course. Please have a seat and I'll summon Mr. Olivier," she said, and picked up the receiver to her phone.

I took a seat in one of the hard-backed leather chairs provided in the waiting area. On the walls hung a pricey collection of art; expensive furniture adorned what little of the offices I could see, and everything was scrupulously clean and orderly. CayBank exuded—in every detail—the right mix of affluence and prudence needed to inspire the confidence of its well-heeled clientele.

Without much delay, a smartly dressed man stepped into the waiting room. As he did I caught in his eye—ever so briefly—the involuntary and scarcely perceptible hint of recognition. The room, which a moment ago was peaceful and inviting, was suddenly filled with tension. Even the receptionist could sense it as she glanced back and forth between the man and me and then pretended to busy herself with something on her desk.

"Hello, sir, welcome to CayBank. I am Janèt Olivier," the man said, graciously extending his hand. He was young, perhaps even younger than me, wearing a perfectly tailored dark blue suit, with blue eyes to match. As his hand extended, he flashed me that condescending smile that the French mastered sometime during the reign of Louis XIV.

Shocked that this Olivier had recognized me, I hesitated. My plan had left a gaping hole and as I stared at Olivier's extended hand I realized my chances of leaving this island alive were taking a nosedive.

Finally, after an awkward moment of indecision, I extended my hand. "Nice to meet you, Mr. Olivier," I said.

"How may we serve you?" he said. His English was flawless but spoken with an ever-so-slight accent.

"Yes. I need to get into my box. My safe-deposit box," I said, showing him the key and then replacing it in my pocket.

"Very well. Your box number?" he said.

"1593," I said. Once again his eyes betrayed him. The number had confirmed it—I was the man he had been expecting.

"Certainly. Please follow me," he said after a brief hesitation. He turned with almost military precision and walked back down the long hallway he had used to enter the lobby. The hallway extended from the reception area in the front of the bank to the rear entry, the second of the only two doors in or out of the building. The long, narrow hall was lit by several wall sconces and featured dark inlaid wood panels and navy carpet. Olivier stopped in the middle of the hall where a single elevator was located and pressed the down arrow.

Entering the elevator, he pushed B. I positioned myself to his right and slightly behind him so I could study his body language as the elevator made its slow descent to the basement. Olivier stood almost at attention, looking straight forward.

As I studied him, my mind was racing. I had not expected these people—whoever they were—to have contacts inside the bank. Cayman Island banks, like Swiss banks, are known the world over for the absolute rock-solid protection and secrecy they offer their clients. I had expected that the bank was being watched, perhaps even electronically. But the complicity of the bank staff was not something I had even considered, much less planned for. Until

Olivier had met me in the lobby, I had been harboring hopes that I might conduct my business on the island without ever being detected.

I now had to formulate and execute a new plan. My mind was racing and drawing a blank at every turn. I was trapped inside the bank, surrounded by enemies intent on killing me, with no idea whatsoever about how to escape. The claustrophobia which tinged me only minutes before was beginning to take root.

The elevator opened on what seemed like an empty room. Stepping out, however, we were greeted by an armed but jovial-looking security guard sitting in the middle of a circular desk at the far end of an elongated room. Behind the desk was the large vault door that lead to the safe-deposit boxes. Although more sparsely decorated than the floors above, this room too was designed to provide the bank's clients with that certain level of comfort. It was twice as wide as it was long, and dominated by the guard's desk. Although well lit, the room had a strange quality about it.

"Janèt, I did not know you were in yet this morning," said the fiftysomething security guard with a chuckle.

"Yes, of course, I am always in by this time," Janèt said, looking at me out of the corner of his eye.

"We will be accessing box 1593 this morning, Mr. Pritchard."

The mention of that box number did not escape Mr. Pritchard's attention, either. His expression turned ominous as he fixed his gaze on me. The guard's overt acknowledgement of me annoyed Olivier.

"*Now*, Mr. Pritchard," he said with a sharpness in his voice that startled both Pritchard and me.

Jumping as if coming out of a daze, Pritchard made a couple of quick entries on the computer keyboard at his fingertips.

"Okay, Mr. Olivier," he said in a more official tone and handed him a group of keys.

Following Olivier, I walked around the desk and through an incredibly thick vault door into a room not unlike what you would find in a library, featuring several rows of shelves. But instead of books these shelves were made of safe-deposit boxes. Olivier walked directly to 1593, which was neither the smallest nor the largest box in the vault. Without saying a word he unlocked his part of the box.

Then turning to me he said, "Your key should do the rest."

I stuck my key in the lock next to the one he had opened. It slid in effortlessly almost as if it wanted to be in the lock. It turned with the smooth, solid feel of a well-made lock, clicking into place after I had turned it an entire three hundred and sixty degrees.

When I removed my key, Olivier grabbed the box by the handle between the two locks, removed it from its place, and said, "Follow me, please."

I followed him into another secure room off the main room which consisted—as Tommy had described—of a small hallway with three doors on either side. Each room, as best I could tell, was about the size of a department store dressing room. He showed me into the first one, which had a small wooden desk and a chair. A light hung from the ceiling to approximately eye level over the center of the small table.

"Please take your time in here. No one will bother you, and when you are done, replace the box in its slot. It will automatically resecure itself. Mr. Pritchard will show you out."

"Yes, thank you," I said as Olivier gave a slight bow and closed the door.

Waiting a second to make sure he was gone I opened the box. In it I found two pairs of diamond earrings and matching necklaces, what looked like about fifty thousand dollars in cash divided into bundles of five thousand, and underneath it all a nondescript CD-ROM. It seemed such an innocent thing just sitting there tucked away in the box, nothing by way of directions either on the disk or in its case. I held the disk up and examined it closely in the light as if looking at it up close would reveal some of its secrets. After I examined the disk as closely as I could, I removed the money from the box and found that several of the bundles were soaked through with blood—dried blood. Those, I decided, would stay in the box. The rest of the money, which amounted to nearly forty thousand, would go out with Tommy.

Just as I was replacing the bloodstained money in the box, I heard Olivier entering the hallway again.

"You are familiar with our procedures?" said Olivier.

"Yeah, sure," Tommy said, and a small wave of relief swept over me.

In a moment Olivier was gone again and there came a very soft knock at my door. "Hank, you in there?" said Tommy in a whisper.

I did not say anything, but quietly opened the door.

"You have any problems?" I said in a barely audible whisper.

"Nope. You?"

"They recognized me," I said, and the fear returned to Tommy's eyes.

"We gotta get outta here, man," he said, reaching for the door.

"No," I said a little louder and a little sharper than I wanted to. "The best thing for us to do is stick to our plan. Besides, your payday just went up. Look at this cash that was in the box," I said, pointing to the cash.

Tommy looked at the cash and then in the direction of the security guard and back again as if he were deciding between the two.

"Tommy, listen to me," I said, grabbing him by both his

shoulders. "Now is not the time to panic. Just take this stuff and go back to the Inn. They don't know you're with me and they are not going to figure it out in the next two minutes."

He nodded slowly before realizing that I was probably right and then said, "Yeah. Okay."

We loaded the cash and jewels into his bag and wedged the disk in his belt directly under his navel.

"Remember, Tommy, if you don't hear from me before morning, call Willie Free at the number I left and get out of here," I said, knowing full well that if he even waited a couple of hours it would be a miracle.

He simply nodded as said, "See you at the plane, man," and left.

Silently I waited. I left the door slightly ajar so I could hear Tommy's exit. Straining, I could hear a brief conversation between him and Pritchard. And then the ding of the elevator calling. I waited another five minutes, which seemed to pass like hours.

Then, leaving the safe-deposit box on the desk and removing my gun from my belt, I walked silently through the vault door. And slowly moved my head around the corner until I could see Pritchard. He was sitting in his chair making a note on a clipboard. I knew there was a panic button somewhere that he could push without me seeing it, so I had to be careful and alert. The moment I stepped from behind the door he would see me and I would still be at least ten feet from him, plenty of time for him to press the button.

Stepping through the door with my gun trained on his head, I said, "Move one muscle, Pritchard, and so help me we will both die down here today." Without a word he dropped his pen and raised his hands above his head without turning around.

"Now, using only your feet, push yourself away from the desk. Slowly."

Gradually his chair began to move backward toward me. When he was far enough away that he could no longer reach any part of the desk, I cautiously approached him, removed his pistol from its holster, and put it in my gym bag.

"Henrie, you don't know what or who you're mixed up with," he said while holding perfectly still.

"I'll grant you that, but if anything happens in this bank you'll be the first casualty," I said, trying to sound like a steely-eyed murderer who would love nothing more than to put a bullet in his head. "But what I want you to do now is to stand up slowly and walk around to the front of the desk."

He stood up and began making his way around the desk. I followed him, making a show of my pistol aimed directly at his head but far enough away the he couldn't knock it out of my hand in one sudden move. Once he was around the desk I removed his handcuffs from his belt and cuffed his hands behind his back. I fished the keys to the cuffs out of his shirt pocket and put them with his gun in my gym bag. Then shoving him as hard as I could, I put his back against the wall in front of the desk and bored my pistol barrel into his forehead.

"Now, Mr. Pritchard, I want you to tell me what I can expect as I try to leave your bank," I said.

"How should I kn—" was all he got out before I brought my knee up into his ribs with all the force I could. He fell to his knees gasping as though he could not catch his breath. I pushed him facedown on the hardwood floor and jammed the barrel of my gun into the back of his head with all my might, pressing his face flat against the floor.

"I mean business here, Pritchard. I'm going to ask this once more and if I don't get a straight answer, the last sound you will ever hear will be the sound of a .45 bullet rattling around inside your skull. Understand?" I said through gritted teeth.

He tried to nod his head but was unable to move so he simply said, "Yes."

"Okay, what can I expect as I leave here?" I said, easing the pressure on the gun.

He turned his head so that he was no longer facedown on the floor and said, "Please, please believe me. All I was supposed to do was to notify Janèt if someone ever came to open box 1593. You've got to believe me, it's all I know," he said.

I pressed the gun down against his temple and slowly cocked the hammer.

"Oh, please. Please, I swear it's all I know. Please, I swear," he said, tears rolling out of his eyes and onto the floor.

"I think you're lying, Pritchard. Let's get that loser Olivier down here and find out, shall we?" I said as I carefully replaced the hammer, pulled him to his feet, and pushed him over to his desk. I reached over his desk and pick up the phone.

"We are going to call Olivier and you are going to ask him to come down here," I said. "What is his extension?"

"129," he said, fighting to regain his composure.

I dialed the number and held the receiver so that I could hear what was said.

"Janèt, I think you better come down here. There is a problem with 1593," he said.

"What kind of problem?" Olivier said, his voiced clearly panicked.

"One your friends will want to know about. Come quickly," he said, and I hung up the phone.

"Very good, Pritchard," I said, bringing the butt of the gun down on the top of his head and allowing him to drop unconscious on the floor.

Thirty seconds later, the elevator dinged. I stood against the wall next to the door so that Olivier could not see me as the door opened.

Before the doors were completely opened he stepped off the elevator and into my hard right hook, knocking him off his feet and back into the elevator. I followed him in and grabbed him by his necktie, delivering a hard kick to the rib cage before dragging him off the elevator again.

Throwing him against the opposite wall, I let loose a flurry of punches to his face and body that left him in a bloody heap at my feet.

Grabbing his hair, I forced him to look over at Pritchard and said, "Your friend is dead and you're next unless I get some answers. What can I expect when I try to leave this bank?" I said, hoping that Pritchard did look dead.

"You can expect to be met by some gentlemen who will insist on relieving you of some sort of disk," he said, wiping away the blood that was running from his nose.

"Do you know how to contact these gentlemen?" I asked.

"Yes, I have only just spoken with them."

"Who are they?"

"People with a lot of money."

I banged his head against the floor, opening a small gash on his forehead.

"Don't give me that baloney, who are they?"

"I don't know. They pay me for information—that's all I know."

"Do you have a car?"

"Of course."

"Where is it parked?"

"In the rear parking lot."

"And that's just outside the back door?"

"Yes."

"How far from the door?"

"One of the reserved stalls, maybe ten meters from the door."

"Take your clothes off," I said, pulling him to his feet.

"Beg your pardon?" he said, truly confused.

"You heard me. Strip to your underwear, we're changing

clothes," I said as I unbuttoned the top two buttons of my
pirate's blouse.

"This is a fifteen-hundred-dollar Armani," he said, examining my clothes to see what he was getting in the bargain.

"Really. How much will an Armani go for with a bul-
lethole in it?" I said.

"Not much, I'm afraid," he said, and began undressing.

A few minutes later I was wearing a suit that was at least
two sizes too small and Olivier was wearing a pirate's costume that was by the same amount too large.

"Now it is time for you to make another call," I said,
pushing him so hard toward the phone that he fell to his
knees. I grabbed his arm and with another hard snatch we
were at the desk.

"Call an ambulance and tell them there has been a shooting," I said, holding the phone up for him to use.

"You must be joking," he said.

"Do I look like I'm brushing up my nightclub act?" I
said, pointing the gun between his eyes.

He made the call, giving the ambulance dispatcher the
information she asked for, and I hung up.

"Now we're going to call your friends and tell them there
was a struggle between me and Pritchard, I'm dead, the
police are on their way over, but you are going to meet
them out front with the disk in two minutes before the
police arrive. And let me warn you, if you so much as clear
your throat in French I'll shoot you in both knees."

He picked up the phone and dialed. Again I held the
receiver so we could both hear.

"Hello," said a man's voice.

"There's been an accident. Pritchard has shot Henrie."

"Why?"

"I can't explain now. Meet me in front before the police
arrive. "I'll have the disk," he said. I could hear the man
start to respond, but I hung up the phone.

"Very good, Olivier. Now empty that trash can in the middle of the room and all the other papers on Pritchard's desk. Fast."

Olivier dumped the trash can, several newspapers, and some other papers in the middle of the room, while I found a lighter in Pritchard's front pocket and set them on fire. A few seconds later there was a roaring fire in the middle of the room and the ceiling-mounted sprinklers and fire alarms were going off.

As the flames burned I called the elevator. By the time it arrived the water had awakened Pritchard and all but extinguished the fire, leaving only a thick layer of smoke. I dragged Olivier to the top floor where confusion reigned as people scrambled to escape the sprinklers and the ear-piercing sound of the fire alarm.

Holding the gun as discreetly as I could, I pushed Olivier from the elevator to the back door. The people pushed by us on either side as they made their exit. From the door I could see a parking lot of about fifty cars. Out of the door streamed the employees of the bank, relieved not so much to be away from a fire, but to be out of the cold sprinkler water.

As we reached the door, I could hear the first sounds of the approaching ambulance. I pushed Olivier out the door first, following close behind. He took a few steps and tripped. I tried to pull him to his feet again but he had gone completely limp. Looking down, I noticed fresh blood on his chest, then I saw the bullet holes—one in his head and two in his chest. Olivier lay shot to death at my feet. Without taking time to look up I dove for cover behind the nearest car.

Peeking over the hood of the car, I tried to see where the shots had come from but I could see nothing through the throngs of people who continued to pour out of the bank. Then I noticed a car in the rear of the parking lot—a car with two men, one of whom appeared to be pointing a pistol in my direction.

Tap-tap-tap came the malignant sound of the bullets fired from a silenced gun as they hit the car I was hiding behind. I ducked behind the car again and began trying to find Olivier's car. I spotted a blue BMW two cars away, about where he said it would be. Just as I began to make my crouched dash for Olivier's car, someone noticed the bullet holes in Olivier's body.

"He's dead. Someone killed Janèt!" yelled a hysterical woman. Immediately the mood of the crowd changed from one of disgust to fear and confusion and panic.

Again I heard the whizzing bullets landing all around me.

Making it to Olivier's car, I was shielded by three cars from the gunman. I worked as fast as I could to get the doors unlocked but managed to trip the theft alarm in the process which only added to the confusion. Getting in, I cranked the car and slammed it into reverse. Seeing an opening in the crowd behind me, I punched the gas, ramming into the car behind me. Putting the car in drive, I tried to pick my way through the crowd.

The gunman got out of his car and ran to intercept my escape. People seeing his gun began to clear him a path as they tripped over each other trying to get out of his way.

"He's got a gun. A gun!" someone screamed.

As people ran from both the building and the gunman, a path began to clear in front of the car. With nothing to lose I ducked my head completely under the dash and floored it. Bullet after bullet ripped through the car. Peeking above the dash for a split second, I swerved out of my path just far enough to hit the gunman, who smashed into the windshield, flew over the top of the car, and fell into a crumpled heap onto the parking lot asphalt.

The windshield was now so shattered I could not see to drive. I started to roll down the window so I could see but noticed it had already been shot out. Sticking my head out the window, I tried to make my way from the rear parking lot to the street in front. The car was making a terrible noise; all the windows and at least two tires had been shot out. The gunman's driver was now out of his car chasing after me on foot with his gun drawn, but having trouble pushing through the panicked crowd. All around me were people yelling, screaming in terror.

As I made it about halfway down the drive leading from the rear parking lot to the street in front, I saw two more men on foot making their way toward me with guns drawn. Like a tidal surge, people were running from the two men who approached from the front. The man advancing from the rear was creating a similar effect. The throng of people were trapped on the drive between the three gunmen. They, in turn, were trapping me, keeping me from moving the car.

My mind was racing and I was fighting hard not to panic.

Reaching into my gym bag I retrieved the decoy disk. I held it out the window high enough for the men to see it. They stopped in their tracks, held up their guns, and tried to get a clean shot at me, which only created more panic in the crowd. I quickly got out of the car, and tossed the disk into the crowd of people. The men, at least temporarily, lost interest in me. Dropping their guns to their sides, they made a scramble for the disk, viciously pushing people out of their way in an attempt to find it.

I pushed through the crowd toward the front of the bank as fast as I could. Once in front of the bank I spotted an empty car parked on the curb with the driver's door opened and the engine running—most likely left by the gunmen.

As I reached the car I looked back. One of the men had broken away from the search for the disk and began pushing through the crowd after me trying to get a clear shot. Sliding into the driver's seat, I shut the door and put the car in drive. As I did, a bullet smashed into the driver-side window. It narrowly missed me, but peppered me with shards of glass, embedding them in my face, neck, and head. My eyelids were full of glass slivers—I could not open them—but I knew the gunman would be on me at any moment. Lying on the horn, I pulled away from the curb, driving blind, praying I didn't hit anyone. Ramming into other cars parked on the street, I desperately tried to wipe the glass from my eyes so I could see. In a moment or two, I had my right eye clear. I hit the gas, looking in my rearview mirror just in time to see the three gunmen running down the street trying to get a clean shot.

I made a right-hand turn on the first cross street and was gone.

Chapter Thirteen

Finding my way to Harbour Drive, I turned north toward Seven Mile Beach. There was a searing pain in my left eye, which I could not open, and I was afraid it was seriously injured. My face was stinging and, as carefully as I could, I removed several larger pieces of glass protruding far enough that I could get my fingers around them.

I found a cell phone in the seat next to me and called the Ambassador Inn and asked for Tommy's room.

"I'm sorry, Mr. Carrera has just checked out," said a young woman, who sounded as though she truly was sorry.

I felt the rage begin to bubble up into my throat. "How long ago did he leave?" I asked through gritted teeth.

"Only ten or fifteen minutes ago. Is there anything I can do to help, sir?"

"No, thank you," I managed to get out before I threw the phone across the car. I had known that Tommy could not be trusted in a crisis, but he had barely had time to get back to the Inn.

I had one chance and that was to catch him at Morgan's Harbour before he took off. Driving as fast as I dared I drove to the Harbour and parked as close as I could to the dock.

Leaving everything but my gun in the car, I ran to the

112

docks and spotted Tommy's bright orange plane as it began to pull away from the dock.

Frantically I ran, each step jarring the glass deeper and deeper into my eye and face. Reaching the end of the dock, I dove into the water. With the salt water stinging my face and eye, I swam as hard as could to catch the plane which was beginning now to pick up a little speed. Exerting what felt like was my last bit of strength, I lunged forward and grabbed the pilot's-side rudder at the tail end of the pontoon. Completely exhausted, I had to take a moment just to hang on while I gathered the strength to pull myself out of the water and onto the pontoon. I knew I had to move quickly, otherwise the plane would be moving so fast I would not be able to pull myself out of the water. Summoning what strength I had left, I pulled myself onto the pontoon, first one leg then the other. Tommy was far enough away from the dock now that I was afraid that if I fell off I would not have the strength to swim back. I was quite literally holding on for dear life and there was not much on the outside of the plane to hold on to. Breath heaving in and out of my chest in rapid succession, digging my fingers into every crack and crevice I could find, I slowly made my way up the side of the plane until I reached the pilot's window seconds before liftoff.

I knocked on the window, scaring Tommy within an inch of his life.

Opening the window, he yelled, "Hank, I thought you were dead!"

"Yeah, right. Stop the plane so I can get in."

He idled down the plane, and I made my way around to the passenger side and used my last bit of energy to crawl in the plane.

"What happened, Hank? I heard all those sirens—"

"Shut up, Tommy, and get us outta here," I said, cutting him off mid-sentence as I leaned back in the chair and shut the door. He began throttling the plane up again.

"What happened to your face, man? It looks like hamburger."

"Just shut up and fly," I said.

A few minutes later we were in the air and headed north. Once Grand Cayman was safely out of sight I relaxed a bit. I tried in vain to find a comfortable position for my back, and used my reflection in the window to get a look at my face and eye. What I could see of my left eye was not encouraging. It was swollen and bright red. My face had several deep cuts and there were several places where pieces of glass were still lodged, but frankly I looked better than I had feared.

"Where's the disk?" I asked after I calmed down a bit.

Tommy reached into the backseat and pulled his overnight bag into his lap and produced the disk from one of the side pockets. I took the disk and held it on my lap for the rest of the flight home.

It was dusk when we docked in Mobile Bay. I called Suzanna from the nearest pay phone.

"I got it," I said after she answered.

"You did?" she said. The excitement in her voice was gratifying. Impressing Suzanna was no easy trick, but I had managed to do it.

"We'll call Cummings when I get there and hopefully make the trade tonight."

"Tonight? Do think that's a good idea?" she said, a little skeptical.

"Sooner the better. I'll see you in a while," I said, and hung up the phone.

Back at Tommy's I found the card I had taken from Cummings's pocket at Blue Springs and dialed the number.

"Hello," said the gravelly voice of an older man.

"I need to speak with Cummings," I said.

"Who's calling?"

"Lafayette Henrie," I said.

"Hang on, I'll patch you through," said the voice.

"This is Cummings," said a voice I recognized from Blue Springs.

"I've got your disk," I said.

"That's a good boy, Lafayette, I knew you could do it. We need to meet. Where are you?"

"Mobile, Alabama."

"Hang on while I grab a map." He put the phone down and I heard the sound of rustling papers.

"Okay, okay. You know where Langan Park is? Intersection of Highway 98 and McGregor Avenue."

"I can find it," I said.

"Meet me there in three hours. I'm going to have to fly in," he said.

"I'll see you there," I said and hung up the phone.

The next order of business was to get my eye taken care of. Jasmine and Suzanna took me to a walk-in clinic not far from Tommy's house in Chickasaw.

While Suzanna and Jasmine waited in the lobby, a twenty-something nurse lead me down a short hallway to a treatment room with a table in its center and a counter along two walls. Other than the examination table, the only furniture in the room was a stool on wheels, an adjustable tray, and a folding chair.

"Take your shirt off and lie down on the table," she said as she removed a pair of latex gloves from a dispenser on the counter. She acted as though she had unexpectedly been called in to work on her night off.

With the gloves on she unbundled some sterile instruments, which had been wrapped in a hospital-green cloth and sealed with an adhesive strip marked STERILE. She placed them on the stainless-steel tray she had positioned close to my face. Without explanation she began examining my eye.

"I don't see any glass but there are some pretty deep cuts in the cornea and serous membrane around the eyeball," she said, but offered no other commentary.

When she finished with my eye she began to remove the bits of glass still lodged in my face, neck, and head. I lay still and let her work, cringing every now and then as she removed one of the bigger pieces.

"Some of these cuts on your face are going to need stitches. Do you want a plastic surgeon?" she said as she dropped one of the bigger pieces in the stainless-steel bowl.

"No, whoever's on duty here will be fine," I said.

She made no reply, but I assumed she had heard my response.

When she finished she removed her gloves, dropped them in a wastebin by the counter, and started making notes on my file.

"The doctor'll be in in a moment," she said, not looking up from her work. After finishing her notations she left.

Ten minutes later she returned with the doctor.

"Hello, Mr . . ." The doctor paused to read my name off the file. "Henrie, I'm Dr. Sands." She was an older woman with short gray hair and a warm smile.

"Lafayette," she said. "That is an interesting first name."

"That's a polite way of describing it," I said.

"Oh, I love it. The world needs more unique names. How did you come by yours?" she said, handing my file to the nurse and devoting her complete attention to me. The nurse rolled her eyes and sat in the room's lone chair.

"My mother, actually. She has a fascination with French history and wanted to give me a French name. And the great Marquis de Lafayette stole her heart. Why she could not at least have gone with Marquis, I still don't understand." As we spoke the doctor held and caressed my hand in hers. Normally this kind of contact with a stranger would make me extremely uncomfortable but with her it was soothing and relaxing.

"You should be grateful she never developed an affinity for Robespierre," she said.

"That thought has crossed my mind many times. Luckily, she was not a fan of the Reign of Terror," I said.

"Indeed. What happened here?" she said, turning her attention to my injuries. Her bedside manner had lightened my mood so much that I had almost forgotten my injuries.

"I was driving down the road and some kid threw a rock and shattered my car window."

"Must have had a pretty strong arm," she said with a skeptical smile.

"Must have," I said, shrugging my shoulders and smiling.

She removed a small pin light from the breast pocket of her lab coat and began to examine my eye.

"I'll clean this up for you and stitch up these other cuts, but you need an eye specialist to look at your eye. I'll have the nurse call the hospital," she said. Her face was close to mine as she examined my eye. I could feel her breath as she enunciated the word "specialist."

"Is it that bad?"

"Could be. I can't say for sure. That's why you need a specialist to look at it," she said.

"I'm going home tonight. Just patch it up and I'll see a specialist tomorrow," I said.

"You need to take care of this immediately. Your eyesight is nothing to play with," she said as she continued her examination.

"Yeah, I know. I promise I'll take care of it first thing in the morning."

She finished her examination and spread fourteen stitches over nine different cuts.

"Don't let me find out that you didn't see a specialist first thing tomorrow morning, Lafayette," she said, patting the back of my hand with her soft hands. "And stay away from those strong-armed kids, too. Next time they might blind you."

Chapter Fourteen

It was a crisp, cool evening in Langan Park. A night that, under different circumstances, could be enjoyed. I had given the disk to Suzanna and she was stationed at a greasy spoon not far from the park with a mobile phone. Once I was sure that Cummings had the information I needed, I would call her and have her bring over the disk.

I arrived at the park early in order to find the best spot. After pretending to leisurely stroll around the park I found a bench that had a good view in all directions, took a seat, and waited.

Ten minutes later two men in business suits emerged from the shadows, walking toward me. As they stepped further into the light, I could see it was Cummings and Banks. They approached without a word and Banks motioned for me to stand up, which I did. Producing some type of electronic wand from his coat, he held it about an inch from my body, waving it all over me from head to toe. Although it was never explained, I assumed they were checking me for a wire.

"He's clean," Banks said to Cummings, and walked away the same way he had come.

"You look terrible, Henrie," Cummings said, looking at my bandaged eye and the sterile gauze wrapped around my head. I made no attempt to respond, but waited for him to take a seat next to me.

"You brought the information?" I asked.

"Do you have the disk?" he said.

"All I've got do is call Suzanna and she's here with the disk in two minutes," I said, holding up a mobile phone.

"Good. That's good. But we've got a problem," he said as his brow furrowed.

"Don't start this with me. We had a deal. I get the disk and you give me the evidence on who killed Stan Tanner," I said, letting the anger rise in my voice.

"First of all, we did not have a deal. You left me face-down in the dirt. Second of all, things have changed. So just calm down and listen to me," he said, looking around to see if we were attracting any undue attention.

For a moment I brooded over whether or not to just get up and leave, but realized no matter how angry I was, listening to him was the best thing to do. Besides, I had nothing else to lose.

"Okay," I said, "make it fast."

"This is going to take some explaining, so keep your shirt on," he said.

"Whatever, Cummings. Let's just hear it," I said, frustrated that I felt compelled to listen to his story.

"Let me preface this whole conversation by saying that the only reason I'm telling you this is that anything I'm about to tell you about our—how shall I say it—activities in this matter can never be proven. Never. We have taken extreme care to see that no evidence exists. So just keep that in mind."

"Who is 'we'?" I said.

"The Central Intelligence Agency. I work for the CIA," he said.

"Figures," I said to let him know that I was not impressed.

"This is a story about industrial espionage. America

doesn't have just one set of enemies anymore. It's much more complicated than that. Much, much more. We are facing significant threats from countries who have absolutely no military designs on us. In fact, some of our biggest threats come from countries that people inside and outside the government think of as our strongest allies. But with the Iron Curtain gone, international trade and global markets have become a far greater concern than Russia or terrorism, really. Yet we are bound in alliances to fight terrorism and military aggression with countries who are our enemies on the economic battlefield. They cooperate with us when it is in their best interest and they don't when it's not.

"We are competing for market share, not military dominance. And our competitive edge is being stolen right from under our noses by people who are supposed to be our friends. The Japanese, the Germans, the French—they all have vast networks of industrial spies in this country. Stealing trade secrets, new technologies, strategic plans, that kind of stuff.

"Ever hear of a Pierre Marion?" he asked abruptly.

"No."

"Don't feel bad, most Americans haven't. When François Mitterand was first elected France's president, he wanted to clean house at French Intelligence, known as the Direction Générale de la Sécurité Extérieure—DGSE for short. So he brought in an old friend, supposed outsider Pierre Marion.

"During his professional career, Marion had been stationed all over the world, including Washington, as an executive for companies like Air France and Aerospace Consortium. But throughout his entire professional career he maintained a clandestine relationship with the DGSE. Marion was what the DGSE called an Honorary Correspondent. Just a fancy name for industrial spy. In his duties as an Honorary Correspondent, Marion spied on his clients, peers in foreign companies, and rival foreign businesses. It was under his direction, for instance, that Air France began electronically eavesdropping on all of its business-class passengers on international flights. Think about that for a second. Air France eavesdrops on every conversation its business-class travelers have.

"Anyway, when Mitterand appointed Marion to head the DGSE, it looked as though he was appointing an outsider, when in reality he was appointing the ultimate insider. Although France had been active in industrial espionage before 1981, Marion significantly upgraded and intensified the DGSE's effort in economic espionage.

"One of Marion's first acts as head of the DGSE was to create an economic espionage division with the agency. He gave this division a blank check. Told 'em they could do whatever they wanted with virtually no oversight of any kind. And believe me, they've been up to their neck in it ever since.

"Their first big success was stealing a two-billion-dollar contract from the U.S. In 1982 we were competing with the Soviet Union and France to sell off some fighter aircraft to India. Through its network of industrial spies in India, the French government got an early look at the American bid. After that they simply undercut the American price and won the bid. Eventually, the Indian Government uncovered the French spy network and fifteen high-ranking officials were arrested. The military attaché who had run the operation for the DGSE was recalled and two other French businessmen barely escaped arrest by fleeing the country.

"In another case French and U.S. companies were bidding against one another to build two nuclear power plants for the government of South Korea. One of the two officials responsible for making the decision on the bid was offered a million dollars in cash and an apartment on the Champs-Élysées if the French company got the bid. You can guess who built the plants.

"Those are just some of their early successes. In the fifteen or so years since then, they have become more aggressive. We have known for some time that they have been constructing a very elaborate and extensive network in this country. Not so much within the government but inside businesses, especially companies involved in high-tech stuff and R & D. And from what we can tell, this network—at least the part that's in the U.S.—is collecting all kinds of information about American companies—business plans, trade secrets, product innovations—and funneling it back to the French government, who is in turn parsing it out to the French companies in direct competition with the companies from whom the information was stolen.

"You with me so far?" he asked, looking at me for the first time since starting the story.

"Yeah, I think I got it. Let me ask you this before you go on. Have the French ever infiltrated a Swiss bank?" I hated to sound interested in his story, but my curiosity got the better of me.

"Oh, yes, many times. The best example of it was one of their failed attempts—those are the only ones you ever learn about anyway. Anyway, back in 1980 they blackmailed a Swiss banker, a guy by the name of Herr Stroehlin of Union des Banques Suisses, or UBS for short. They put together this elaborate scheme to make it look like he had stolen a car. They offered to drop the matter if he would provide the DGSE with a list of UBS's names and numbered accounts. Stroehlin was quick on his feet and told the French authorities that he did not have access to such information, but that if they were willing to pay he knew someone that could and would. The DGSE agreed. When they met in Zurich to make the trade, the DGSE agent was confronted by a swarm of Swiss police officers and arrested. So yes, banks are infiltrated all the time. I heard you had some trouble with CayBank."

"Nothing I couldn't handle," I said.

"Should I continue?" he asked.

"Suit yourself," I said, back to being interested.

"Okay, Stansfield Tanner. About two years ago, by sheer accident we uncovered a French spy inside TaraTech, Tanner's company. My predecessor met with Stan and showed him what we had. You can imagine, Stan was furious. The person had access to his most sensitive information. It was all we could do to keep Stan from creating an international incident. Finally, after several months of working with him we convinced him to help us uncover the entire network. At our suggestion, he opened an office in Paris.

"Meanwhile, this spy was none the wiser and continued to pass information back to the DGSE, but since we could control the information she had access to, we controlled what the DGSE saw. When we wanted the French to know something we would allow her to 'discover' it.

"Eventually the mole tipped her hand to us. We intercepted a communiqué from her handler that revealed their true goal of stealing TaraTech's advanced encryption processes. So we let the mole discover that Stan might be interested in doing business with the DGSE. Two months later, an agent of the DGSE approached Tanner at a Paris café and our little sting operation was under way.

"We were handicapped by Tanner's lack of experience and training but he learned quickly. Stan's objective was to find someone inside the DGSE who could provide information on the DGSE's activities in the U.S. We never imagined he would have the success he had. Frankly, his success is what has put this whole operation in jeopardy, but I'll get to that in a minute. Stan found someone who could not only give us information, but was willing to provide us with the list of their entire U.S. network—everybody. The price was extremely high, but it was an offer we could not refuse.

"We got the money and Stan went to Zurich to make the trade. But somewhere there was a breakdown or leak or something, and at the last moment DGSE discovered our plan. To this day we are not sure what happened, but this much we know. Stan escaped with minor injuries and the encrypted list on the CD-ROM. Stan's mole inside the DGSE is dead. Our man on the ground in Zurich died in a car accident in Frankfurt. And Stan's handler here, the guy who ran this operation before me, drowned in a boating accident. Both accidents on the same day the deal went bad in Zurich. Imagine the coincidence.

"Anyway, Stan was in the cold, so to speak, for a few weeks while we tried to figure out what happened. That's what I meant when I said his success has jeopardized the operation. My bosses had become concerned that the deal Tanner had made was too good. They didn't believe that anybody, much less an amateur, could get that kind of information from the DGSE. They were concerned that Tanner had deceived us into giving him the money while making it appear that the deal went south so he could keep the money himself.

"So Stan was in the cold and feared for his life. With good reason, I guess," he said with about the same remorse you feel while watching the sun set.

"He didn't like having the disk around, you know, while things were being sorted out," he continued. "So he put the disk in his Grand Cayman safe-deposit box.

"Eventually, we were able to confirm Tanner's innocence through independent sources, and we reestablished contact. Stan was livid—well, you can imagine how he felt. By the time we calmed him down, Suzanna had stolen the key from him. He was trying to get the key back when the boys from the DGSE paid him a visit.

"Here's the funny thing," he said, and actually chuckled. "If you and Suzanna hadn't been trying to steal her jewelry that night, right now you'd be back in Marianna doing whatever it is you do and she would be just as dead as Stan. So in a way your greed saved her life."

"And almost cost me mine," I said, more to myself than to Cummings. " 'Course, if you guys hadn't been so paranoid you'd have your list and Suzanna and I wouldn't even be involved in this thing," I said after thinking about it for another second.

"Yes, that's another way to look at it," he said, nodding his head.

"This is all very interesting, but I don't see how it affects me."

"Right. That was all background on our little problem. Somehow the FBI got wind that Stan is selling this militarily sensitive information to the DGSE and they started their own investigation. But like I said earlier, our tracks are covered so they never saw the CIA in it. All they ever saw was a greedy businessman selling out his country for money. They had their sights locked on Tanner and never even suspected we were involved. Stan never really planned to transfer the information to the DGSE and the FBI never had enough to indict him," he said.

"Again, very interesting. And don't get me wrong, I'm enjoying learning how you guys screwed this thing up and got Stan and two of your own guys killed, but I still don't see how it affects me," I said.

"Okay, okay. Just bear with me a minute longer. The disk, the one you've got, is encrypted. It's useless to us unless it's decrypted. We had a couple of other contacts inside TaraTech who could do it for us. But now that the FBI is investigating Stan's murder, they've cut off all contact with us," he said.

"Why in the world would they do that?" I said.

"The FBI hasn't been able to confirm that there is a CIA operation," he said, studying my body language very closely.

"Why don't you—the CIA—just tell the FBI what you're up to, and everybody's problems are solved," I said, completely exasperated.

"Once again Henrie, it's not that simple."

"Spit it out, Cummings, or whatever your name is. What is the problem?" I said.

"Well, the FBI is right, officially our little operation does not exist. To run an operation like this against one of our strongest 'allies' "—he used the index and middle fingers of each hand to indicate the quotation marks around the word "allies"—"we'd need permission from the State Department and the National Security Council, and there is no way they would have signed off on anything like this. They don't want to know if there's a problem, because they don't want to have to deal with the problem. So we've kind of been doing it under the radar so to speak."

"In other words, you are the ones who are freelancing."

"In a manner of speaking. But here is the problem at least as far as you're concerned. Our tracks are covered— completely covered." He paused for emphasis. "The FBI's been all over this thing for a year and they don't suspect a thing. Far as the FBI is concerned, Stan was a traitor. But even they will tell you they never had enough to indict him, much less our other two contacts. Who, squeamish though they are, figured out that all they got to do is keep their mouths shut and they skate. The French? They've done the math, too, and they know they've got the perfect scapegoat for the murder in you. All they have to do is destroy the disk and they skate, too. But they have a slight advantage on me. They don't need it decrypted; they just need it gone. For it to be any good to me it's got to be decrypted."

"How's a decrypted disk going to help you? You still broke the law," I said as I fantasized about strangling him with my bare hands.

"Well, it's a little like breaking-and-entering to catch a murderer. If you catch the murderer everything's fine— you're a hero. If you don't catch him then all you've done is commit a felony. You follow?"

"Unfortunately I do. Either you guys hit a grand slam or you're going to deny you were even at the ballpark," I said.

"Rotten for you. But what can I say . . . you're right," he said. If he had any problems about letting me take the rap for a murder he knew I didn't commit, I couldn't see it.

"So why are you here talking to me?" I asked.

"There is still a way for both of us to get what we want," he said.

"And that is?"

"We believe Suzanna can get the disk decrypted."

"You guys are idiots. She doesn't even know what Stan did for a living," I said.

"Come on, Henrie. You don't think she knows somebody at that company that would help her?"

"I'm telling you she knows squat. Nothing. Everything I know about this situation I learned elsewhere. She is absolutely helpless," I said.

"Henrie, think about it. She was married to the owner of the company. She's got to know somebody. I'm going to write a name down, have her start with him," he said. He ripped a piece of paper from a small pad he had in his front pocket and wrote a name on it.

Holding it out to me he said, "Take it."

I looked back and forth between the paper and Cummings. I never in my life hated anyone the way I hated him at that moment. The idea of strangling the life out of him was seeming more and more reasonable. Even in a fit of rage, I was too tired and spent to actually carry through with it. Nevertheless, I indulged the fantasy.

"Take it, Henrie. What choice do you have?" he said, shoving the paper in my shirt pocket.

Chapter Fifteen

"How'd it go?" Suzanna said when she picked me up about a block from the park.

"Not good, I'm afraid," I said, getting into the Chevy.

We drove around as I told her everything Cummings had said.

"You mean Stan was working for the CIA the whole time?" she said with a laugh after I had related the story.

"I guess so. You're not nearly as mad as I was when I found out about this."

"I'd be furious if I didn't know someone who'd decrypt that disk," she said with a smile.

"Cummings said this Steve Conroy is the guy who could make it happen," I said, holding the paper he had given me up so the I could read in the headlights of the car behind us.

"That guy's a jerk. He's not going to help us. He does nothing but protect his own rear. Stan used to hate that guy. I mean he absolutely loathed him. Don't worry, I know just the person to help us."

When we got back to Tommy's house it was well after midnight. Suzanna went into the front room to collect our few things and I went back to Tommy and Jasmine's bedroom to say good-bye and thank you.

128

Both Tommy and Jasmine were fast asleep. I didn't want to startle him so I gently shook his shoulder. It didn't work. He bolted straight up out of bed as if I had thrown a bucket of cold water on him.

"Wha . . . what's going . . . Gee, Hank, you just about gave me a heart attack. Is there a problem?" he said. Jasmine must have been a hard sleeper, because she remained on her stomach, mouth open, snoring.

"We're leaving, Tommy. I just wanted to thank you for your help," I whispered.

"Listen, Hank." He put his hand on my shoulder and I could see the moonlight glisten on a tear forming in his eye. "I want to apologize again. You're the first person that's come to me in a long time for help, and I let you down. I don't know, I guess I panicked or something—" He dropped his head into his hands.

"Don't mention it again. We got the disk, the jewelry, the money, and we got out alive. Everything worked out just fine," I said.

"That's nice of you to say, Hank. I wish it were true," he said, looking up at me again.

"It's fine, really. I'll call you when I get all this worked out," I said.

It was after 1:00 A.M. when we got on I-65 north headed for Atlanta. As the light of Mobile faded behind us, I lay my head on the tattered headrest and closed my eyes. My back, eye, and face were throbbing in unison. Every bump in the road brought a new adventure in pain.

"This thing sure doesn't handle as well as my Mercedes," Suzanna said.

"Well, this car cost about as much as the hubcaps on your 750," I said.

"You look tired," she said.

"The only decent sleep I've gotten since this whole thing started was the nap I had after Jasmine's massage the other day," I said. Sleep deprivation was beginning to win out over the pain and I was finding it literally impossible to keep my eyes open.

"This is a real easy trip, Suzanna. All you've got to do is stay on I-65 until you get to Montgomery. In Montgomery, get on I-85 and take that on into Atlanta," I think I said with my eyes closed and head on the headrest.

I think she said something about having it under control and that I should get some sleep, but I can't remember.

Suzanna woke me about six hours later just outside of Atlanta.

"We are almost there, sugar," she said, giving me a nudge.

It was almost 8:00 and we had just turned off I-285 and were headed north on I-75 toward Marietta, a suburb north of Atlanta. My back felt a little better, but my eye and face throbbed with pain.

I used the rearview mirror to examine my face. The cuts and scratches not covered by bandages were red and swollen and looked as though they needed a good cleaning.

"Don't take this the wrong way, Hank, but you look bad. How's your back?" Suzanna said.

"Well, hey, listen, I feel like I was just elected prom queen," I said. "I'll be all right as soon as we get this disk decrypted," I added as an afterthought more to myself than to Suzanna.

"Well, that won't be long now. We'll be at Paul's in just a minute," she said.

A minute or two later she pulled off the interstate.

Paul Anglin, Suzanna explained, was a friend—her only friend at TaraTech—who had always been nice to Suzanna, and she was sure that he would be willing to help.

Within a few minutes she pulled the Chevy into the driveway of a big, beautiful home about a mile off of Macland Road. I got out of the car as Suzanna was fixing her hair and makeup in the rearview mirror. Paul's house was nothing on the order of Stan's, but it wasn't a homeless shelter either. Rather new—it looked as though it had been built in the last ten years—it featured a high-pitched roof, used brick with white trim, and was situated in the middle of a neighborhood of similarly styled homes.

"Ready?" Suzanna said. I detected a certain excitement in her voice.

"Why are you looking at me that way?" she said.

"What way?" I realized that I must have been staring. Her whimsical mood seemed out of place considering our situation, but I saw no reason to discuss it with her. I would just add this to the ever-growing list of things about Suzanna which I didn't understand.

"Then stop looking at me like that," she said, reverting just that quickly back to spoiled parvenu.

"After you," I said, stepping aside so that she could lead the way up the walk to the front door. Which she did.

The door was double-wide and white-painted oak with a huge brass knocker which Suzanna used.

Within seconds I could hear anxious footsteps approaching the door. It opened.

"You're okay! I have been worried sick," Paul said as he reached out and pulled Suzanna to him, giving her a longing kiss. At first Suzanna submitted but then abruptly pulled away from him and stole a sideways glance at me. The surprise on my face must have been evident, but I thought it best to let it go without comment. There was an awkward moment in which no one was sure what to say.

Paul was young. Maybe even ten years younger than me. Tall, pale, and skinny, he wore his hair combed straight back and cut to one length a few inches above his shoulder.

"Paul, this is Hank Henrie. He's been helping me," she said. Paul, who was clearly relieved to see Suzanna, seemed surprised to see me.

"Yes, I've heard about you. The two of you . . . on the

news. Come in, come in," he said, holding his hand out and looking back and forth between Suzanna and me as if he did not quite know what to do. After a brief hesitation he opened his door wide enough for us to enter.

I followed Suzanna into the house.

"I was just having some cold cereal. Can I offer you some?"

"Sounds good," I said. "Thank you."

Suzanna and I followed him toward the rear of the house and into a marbled kitchen. Paul showed us to a couple of seats at a bar and got out two bowls and spoons. The kitchen was a mess, not necessarily with dirty dishes, but junk. On the floor by the table were two stacks of newspapers at least three feet tall. Stack upon stacks of mail sat on the counter apparently unopened, and what looked like work papers strode haphazardly on the table and bar. Paul made no apologies; he simply cleared off a place for us to eat and sat the bowls down in front of us.

I was anxious to get down to business, but I wanted to see first if I could verify anything Cummings had told me the night before.

"What's going on at TaraTech now after Stan's death?" I asked.

"Couple of the top guys have taken leaves of absences. Other than that can't really tell much of a difference," he said as if the receptionist had just submitted his resignation.

"The FBI been in to talk to anybody?" I asked.

"They came in with a lot of search warrants, took a lot of stuff, mostly computer files and stuff. Our general counsel says it's routine in a murder investigation."

"Any other rumors?" I asked.

"There are a lot of rumors, but you two are pretty much the hot item," he said.

"What about these guys on leave—any rumors about them?" I said.

"About them killing Stan?" he said, genuinely confused.

"No, excuse me, I didn't mean to imply that. I mean that they may have been involved in something with Stan. Maybe something that got Stan killed."

"Well, right after the FBI guys left they circulated a memo around the office forbidding us from talking about the murder investigation amongst ourselves and especially to anyone outside the company. They said that until the FBI finishes their investigation there would be a lot of rumors and that we didn't want to be part of starting or spreading them. And that anyone caught spreading rumors would be summarily dismissed. So no, there are not a lot of overt rumors swirling around," he said, setting a carton of milk and a box of Lucky Charms in front of me.

"So you don't hear much?" I said, perhaps prying a little further than I should have.

"All I hear is bits and pieces, but for the most part I just keep my head down and do my job," he said.

"The guys on leave figure into those bits and pieces?" I asked, helping myself to a heaping bowl of cereal.

"There are always rumors about the Triangle," he said.

"The Triangle?"

"Yeah, that's what we call Stan, John Tait, and Mel Neyburg—the two guys on leave—the Triangle. They run TaraTech. Stan's the Chairman and CEO. Tait's the Chief Operating Officer and Neyburg the Chief Financial Officer. Their offices are situated around a triangular shaped reception area—thus the Triangle." Paul explained.

It sounded as though what Cummings had told me could be true, Tait and Neyburg were on leave, ostensibly to mourn, but more likely under the direct care and keeping of a high-priced criminal defense attorney in downtown Atlanta. From what Paul explained of the memo, it also sounded like they were telling anybody and everybody who may have had some understanding or idea of what they were doing with the CIA that they should just sit down and shut up and this whole thing would blow over. Trouble was that the whole thing was blowing over on me and it was time to get to business.

"We hate to barge in on you like this, Paul. But we need some help and Suzanna says you're the guy who can help us," I said, ready to get this whole thing over.

"She does, does she?" he said, shooting a questioning glance at Suzanna as though she had revealed some dark secret from his past.

"I don't know what you need, but if I can help count me in," he said, looking back at me.

While we ate, I explained to Paul everything that had happened since Suzanna had showed up at my trailer. Paul was attentive to everything I was saying and didn't have many questions. Suzanna just ate her cereal apparently content to let me tell the story.

"So you have the disk," he said to Suzanna after I had finished the story.

"We've got it," she said. "It just needs to be decrypted."

"Suzanna was right," Paul said to me this time. "You have come to the right place. Give me the disk. I'll take it into the office and be back with the decrypted version in an hour or so."

"That's great, Paul. It's nice of you to help us this way. And I don't want to sound ungrateful, but that disk is not leaving my sight. Where it goes, I go," I said.

"Well, it's Saturday, so there won't be anybody at the office, but the security is pretty tight there. I know how you feel, I'm sure I'd feel the same way, but I'm telling you the safest way is for me to go alone," Paul said, looking at Suzanna for support.

"It'll be all right, Hank, really," Suzanna said, reaching over to pat my hand.

"I'm sure it will be, but I'm not letting that disk out of my sight. I'm not trying to be a jerk here, but that's all there is to it," I said. "If you can't help us I can understand that. I'll have to find someone else, that's all."

"Whoa, whoa," Paul said, holding his hand up as if to say "stop." "I'll help you. Just calm down, cowboy."

"Hank, relax a bit," Suzanna said under her breath, looking at Paul as if she were embarrassed for me.

"Look, I'm sorry, I've been through a lot and I've got too much riding on this disk, that's all," I said.

"Hey, no problem," Paul said with a smile.

After I finished eating Paul showed me to a guest bathroom and offered me some clean clothes—the only thing that fit was the shirt. I took a quick shower being careful not to wet the bandages around my head.

As I turned off the shower I could hear Paul and Suzanna having a heated discussion, although I couldn't make out exactly what it was about. It ended as soon as they realized the shower was off. I decided that Paul was mad at Suzanna for putting him in this situation, but had been too polite too say anything about it in front of me.

With a bottle of peroxide and a few dozen cotton balls I cleaned my cuts. I found an unopened bottle of Motrin in the medicine cabinet, but at closer examination revealed that it was several months past its expiration date. Undaunted, I opened the bottle and took five. I dressed again and joined Suzanna and Paul in the kitchen. There was a tension in the room that had not been there when I left. Paul, who was now dressed in jeans and a button-up shirt, was loading his dishwasher while Suzanna sat at the table with her arms folded. Neither was talking. I put it down to the fight they had obviously had while I was bathing and acted as though I didn't notice.

"Ready?" Paul said after a moment.

"Whenever you are," I said after Suzanna did not answer.

Chapter Sixteen

T he ride to TaraTech was tense but thankfully short. The weather, which had been sunny when we first arrived in Atlanta that morning, had taken a turn for the worse and a brisk rain started falling during the drive over. I rode in the backseat of Paul's car while he drove and Suzanna rode in the passenger seat.

I could not help feeling like I was the reason for all the tension. But I was well past the point of caring about anything like that. I just wanted to get the disk decrypted and get this ordeal over with.

TaraTech, which consisted of a campus of buildings just off I-75 between Marietta and Atlanta, was understated if anything. One small monument sign and flagpole in front was all that welcomed visitors. The campus consisted of seven or eight red brick buildings each no taller than four stories—except for the one in the center, which stood six stories tall. The buildings were all uniform in design, but some were visibly older than others. I guessed they had been built as needed over a twenty-year period.

Using a security card and a pass code, Paul got us into the executive parking lot underneath the main building. Showing us to the elevator, Paul pushed the button for the top floor, where we were greeted again by an electronic gatekeeper requiring the use of Paul's voice, fingerprint, and several security codes to get us through.

Once through the security we walked down a wide hall-way leading to a door marked *Executive Research and Development*. The door opened into a circular common room ringed by five offices and consisting of secretarial desks and a small waiting area. One of the offices we entered was marked *Paul Anglin, Assistant Vice-President for Development*.

"Have a seat," Paul said after clearing a couple of seats for us on a leather sofa. "This will only take a few minutes."

Suzanna and I took a seat. There was an edginess about Suzanna that I could not attribute to the argument with Paul. Putting people in difficult and uncomfortable situa-tions is not something that bothers people like Suzanna. Whatever they want, whatever they ask for, they believe they are entitled to it and act accordingly. They rarely, if ever, stop to consider the inconveniences they impose on their friends and acquaintances. For instance, Suzanna had never once apologized for getting me into this mess and frankly, I never expected her to. That was why her current anxiety level puzzled me.

"Relax, Suzanna, this is almost over," I said, patting her on the knee. She simply nodded her head and avoided mak-ing eye contact with me.

Paul was at his computer working away. His fingers danced across his keyboard with precision, keystroke after keystroke.

The office was big—too big—and in a bigger mess than his house. It was obvious that the only space that was ever used was the leather chair at his desk and the computer. Every other inch of the office was stacked deep with junk. Some of it, in the furthest reaches of the office, slumbered under a visible layer of dust. In the chair where I now sat had been a stack of computer game magazines. The one on top was six months old.

Suzanna and I sat quietly while he worked. And waited.

"Okay, just one more second while it decrypts," his said, hitting the ENTER key with a little extra flair.

Numbers and letters were flashing in across the screen with blinding speed, then—just as suddenly as it began— it stopped and a message appeared on the screen:

CORRECT KEY LOCATED
DECRYPTION SUCCESSFUL

Paul examined the document closely. Using the arrow keys on his keyboard, he quickly moved up and down the document.

"This is it." he said to Suzanna as if I were not in the room. "You've done it. This is the list." Suzanna did not look up, but Paul was elated.

"Great," I said and picked up the receiver to the phone on his desk to call Cummings.

"What do you do to get an outside line?" I said.

"Who do you think you're calling?" Paul said abruptly, and reached to open a desk drawer.

"My contact at the CIA. I'm putting an end to this thing," I said, unable to keep the puzzled look off my face.

As I was saying it, he pulled a gun from his desk and aimed it at me. My first reaction was more anger than fear. I closed my eyes and shook my head as though my eyes were deceiving me. But when I reopened them there he was, holding a gun on me. I could actually feel my blood pressure rising and could taste the bile bubbling up in the back of my throat.

"What's going on here, Suzanna?" I said, grabbing her arm and forcing her to her feet.

"Paul, he's done so much, can't we let him have part of this?" she said, still refusing to look at me.

I looked at Paul. I learned something at that moment. It is hard to be afraid of a computer geek, even when he is pointing a gun at you. Paul could sense that I was not afraid of him and it was beginning to make him nervous. I glared at him while weighing my options and decided now was not the time to move on him. I knew he would make a mistake and when he did I'd snap his pencil-thin neck in two.

"Hank, I tried to let you down gently, but you had to come. Couldn't let that disk out of your sight," he said, almost apologizing.

Ignoring him, I shook Suzanna by both arms. "What is this, Suzanna? What are you doing—what have you done to me?" I said.

"Paul, listen to me, please," Suzanna said. "We need Hank. You heard what he's been through to get the disk—he deserves something. Look at him."

"We don't need him now, Suzanna. He's done everything he can for us. Letting him in was never was part of our deal, and I am not going to let him in now. No way. Let's go," Paul said, trying to be all business.

Using one hand to work the computer and the other to hold the gun on me, Paul printed out a document and put the printout and the disk in a manila envelope, which he tucked under his shirt and into his belt in the small of his back.

"Okay, here is what we are going to do—"

"Please, Paul—" Suzanna said.

"Shut up, Suzanna. Everything is going to be fine if you just shut up," Paul said. The tension was already getting to him.

Tears began running down Suzanna's cheeks. I was finding it hard to work up any sympathy for her.

Turning his attention back to me, Paul said, "You are going to lead the way out of here, to the elevator. We'll take it back down to the parking garage."

Putting his coat on carefully and sliding the gun in the pocket, he said, "Let's go," and motioned me toward the door with the pocketed gun. I walked out of his office and down the hall toward the elevator. Paul made Suzanna walk behind him and he stayed far enough behind me that he would have time to shoot me if I tried anything. I pushed the elevator button and got on when it arrived.

Paul tried to console Suzanna who appeared on the verge of a nervous breakdown, but never took his eyes off me as the elevator descended to the parking garage.

I said nothing but let the hate pour through my eyes as I stared at him. He tried to match my intense stare, but didn't have the nerve for it.

"Okay, now slowly over to the car," he said when the doors opened.

I walked over to his car, which was not far from the elevator. Suzanna had managed to get herself somewhat under control but as we walked out of the building was starting to cry again.

When we got to the car, Paul opened the trunk and fished around for a roll of duct tape. He looked at me and then the tape and realized he had a problem. How was he going to secure my hands? He couldn't have Suzanna hold the gun on me, that much was clear. And to tape my wrists together would require two hands. Holding the gun on me, he took Suzanna and led her to the passenger seat.

"Facedown on the ground," he said to me after the door was shut.

I didn't move but stared at him, daring him to make me get on the ground. The entire garage was quiet except for the sound of my breath whistling through my gritted teeth.

"We're going to do this right here, then," he said, raising his pistol and taking aim at my head.

I continued to stare, thinking that I preferred a bullet to submission. But thankfully that thought passed and reason reasserted itself and with some difficulty I did manage to get on the ground.

Then holding his gun with one hand, he taped my ankles together.

"Now put your hands behind your back," he said.

When I did, he carefully approached my hands and as best he could wrapped them with tape while still holding the gun on me. When he was confident I could not move them, he put his gun down and finished the job.

"Okay, tough guy, on your feet," he said, pulling me to my feet and then taping my mouth shut with four rings of tape wrapped tightly around my head. Then without warning he pushed me headfirst into the trunk of his car and shut it. Clearly, he felt more confident now that my hands and feet were bound.

I could hear his footsteps as he walked around the car, opened the driver's side door, and got in.

"Suzanna, you have got to get yourself under control," he said, shutting the car door mid-sentence.

"What are you going to do with him?" she said.

"If you cared what happened to him then, you should have dumped him the minute he got the disk. That was always the plan. But you didn't, did you? No. You brought him to me. Now I've got to deal with him." He was a real tough guy now.

For several minutes I lay still and tried to hear what they were saying, but it was no use. With the engine running I could not make out what they were saying.

The frustration—the pure rage—I felt in that trunk cannot be described in words. It so consumed me that it nearly rendered me incapable of any rational thought.

I was much too angry to think clearly and I needed to calm down and devise a plan. Being used in the way that Suzanna had used me was not something that you can get over in a matter of minutes. And it is impossible to think clearly when you are as angry as I was at that moment.

What made me even angrier was the fact that I had bought her act from beginning to end. *"I just want my jewelry."* *"He has no right to keep it from me."* *"I'm sorry, Hank, I just don't know what Stan did for a living."* *"I think they may be after the key."* *"I think we'd better get that disk, don't you, Hank?"* Even with Willie trying his best to warn me that something about Suzanna was wrong, I let her lead me like a lamb to the slaughter. It all went over my head. Even when—after strongly protesting that she didn't know anybody or anything about TaraTech—she came up with Paul as someone who could decrypt the disk, still it had not registered with me that she was lying.

Thinking about all her lies and deceptions and my credulous faith in her was not lowering my blood pressure. But gradually I willed that out of my mind and concentrated on the situation at hand.

The first priority was to free my feet and hands. I had already begun trying to get my hands around to the front of my body, by bringing them round under my feet. It was not easy, especially with the condition of my back. I scrunched myself into the tightest ball I could get into and began working my hands down the back of my legs. Pushing, pulling, and straining with all my strength, I could not get my hands under my feet. Finally, I decided I would have to take my shoes off in order to get my hands under.

Even after kicking my shoes off, I nearly could not do it. I pulled and strained so hard against the tape I could feel it cutting into my skin. If it had not been for the absolute necessity of the situation I would not have been able to do it. Finally, I worked my hands under my feet and around to the front of my body.

Next, I began to get the tape off my feet, which was relatively simple once I found the tape's end. With my hands in front and my feet free I began looking for something I could use to cut the tape off my hands. Searching around the spare tire, I found a tire iron that came to a point at one end and was just sharp enough that with some effort could do the job.

I was getting the tire iron situated in my hand when Suzanna screamed, followed a split second later by a violent crash sending me flying across the trunk headfirst. Before I could get my hands up I slammed headfirst into the side of the car.

I must have lost consciousness for a second, because the next thing I was aware of was Suzanna screaming Paul's name over and over again, her voice riddled with panic.

Then I heard a man's voice yelling, *"Quelqu'un a fermé cette femme."*

"Il n'est pas ici," another voice said from inside the car.

Shaking the cobwebs out of my head, I began to search for the tire iron again, thinking that I might need it to defend myself. I found it as someone began trying to open the trunk. Gripping the tire iron with my bound hands, I realized that there was not enough room to get a good swing while lying in the trunk. Dropping the iron, I lay on my side and waited for the trunk to open.

When it did I delivered the hardest kick I could to the chin of the dark-suited man who opened the trunk. Without knowing what hit him, his head took a violent snap backward and he dropped like a wet rag onto the road. It wasn't until my foot struck the man's face that I remembered I was without my shoes. But I could not stop to worry about that now. I was still bound at the wrist, gagged, and blind in one eye by the bandage wrapped around my head.

I fought hard against panic. I was scared to raise my head out of the car and I was scared not to. I had no idea what waited for me, but I had seen the DGSE's handiwork and at the thought of it I began yanking against the tape on my wrist. The tape dug deeper and deeper into my skin, but it was to no avail. I could not get it off. How would I defend myself with my hands bound?

Suzanna continued to scream, but her voice was being muffled—probably by someone's hand.

I peeked over the edge of the trunk; the man I had kicked was out cold on the pavement. A gun lay a few feet from his side. As yet, no one had seemed to have noticed what happened to him. Looking quickly and cautiously around I saw a dark-colored Suburban wrecked into the side of Paul's car. We were in the middle of a residential street, which I guessed was not far from Paul's house. What other men there were must have been searching Paul's car, because I could not see them, but I could feel the car move as they moved about inside the vehicle.

Springing from the car, I grabbed the gun lying on the road and rolled quickly to the passenger side of the car, where I startled a man in a suit holding a gun in one hand and trying to control Suzanna with the other. He was standing by the open passenger door and pulling Suzanna out. Seeing me he raised his gun and pulled Suzanna closer so he could use her as a shield.

I rolled back to the rear of the car as two bullets ricocheted off the pavement where I had been lying.

"Henrie est par le joncteur réseau," he shouted, and drug Suzanna toward the Suburban.

I lay flat on my stomach so I could see their feet as they walked. After Suzanna was in the Suburban, a foot came out of Paul's car. Without even a moment's hesitation I shot it right in the ankle. It was the first time I had ever shot anyone with a silenced gun and it made a grisly thud which was followed by an agony-ridden scream from inside the car.

"J'ai été projectile, il m'a tiré dans la chevill!" he yelled.

The man who had put Suzanna in the Suburban was trying now to get back to the car. I tried to shoot him in the ankle, too. Even though I missed and hit the car's tire, it was enough to cause him to retreat.

Just then I heard the back window of the car shatter as someone busted it out and crawled out onto the trunk. Raising my gun over the trunk I fired several blind shots into the car. As I did, I could see the man's feet by the Suburban as he started making a run in my direction. Pulling the gun back down I managed to shoot him just below his right knee when he was about halfway between the Suburban and the car. He hit the ground rolled up into a ball with both hands on his leg, blood trickling between his fingers and down his leg.

His gun fell a few feet from me. Carefully, I reached out and grabbed it. I thought for a second about killing the man as he writhed in pain, but even though I knew he would not extend me the same leniency, I could not bring myself to do it.

All was quiet for a minute except for the moans of the two men I had shot. Cautiously I raised my head above the trunk. A man—by all appearances dead—lay sprawled over it. Another man sat in the front seat half holding a gun in my direction half trying to look after his ankle.

Staying in a crouched position, I scurried around to the passenger's side door. The man whom I had shot in the ankle, was sitting with his back toward me facing the Suburban, unaware that I was behind him. With all my might I tried one more time to free my hands from the tape. Again I failed.

"Derrière vous, Jean!" yelled the man I had shot in the shin.

But it was too late, holding the gun in one hand and his shirt collar in the other I snatched the man out of the car and onto the ground. He screamed in agony as he hit the ground and dropped his gun in favor of grabbing his ankle. I kicked the gun as far away as I could and climbed into the car.

Paul was leaning back against the seat with his head on the rest as if he were taking a nap. He was dead. One shot to the head had finished him. He still held the gun he must have pulled out when the men approached. Pushing his lifeless body forward onto the steering wheel, I removed the envelope from his back. As I did another bullet smacked into his body. Instinctively I dove for cover on the floorboard of the car. Several more bullets ripped through the car.

They were coming from the direction of the Suburban but I was sure no one but Suzanna was in it. Keeping myself down I backed out of the car. The man I had left holding his ankle was crawling toward his gun. Unable to contain my anger any longer I snapped. In sheer rage I delivered several blows to his face and head with the butt of my pistol. With my wrist taped together I could not get any force behind my blows, so their only effect was to sap me of what little strength I had remaining. Chest heaving for breath, I crawled off the man and brought the barrel of my gun to his forehead.

Calmly he stared at me. I was tightening my grip on the trigger when I heard the sound of sirens as they began to approach from several different directions. Releasing my grip on the trigger, I drew the gun away from the man's head. I knew I could not afford to leave a trail of dead bodies in my wake. Catching my breath again I crawled the few feet back over to the car. Peeking over, I could see the man who I had shot in the shin now in the driver's seat of the Suburban holding a gun out the window.

The instant he saw me he fired off four more rounds in my direction. I started to return fire but realized I might hit Suzanna. Then I wondered why I even cared.

"Henrie, we need the disk. This is all," the man in the Suburban yelled in stilted English.

The sirens were getting closer and I knew whatever I did it would have to be done quickly. Sitting behind the passenger side front tire I was racking my brain trying to come up with a plan.

"Il n'y a aucun disque dans la voiture!" the man beside on the ground yelled.

"Donnez-moi une seconde au rampement loin et à l'explosion la voiture. Elle le détruira. Nous pouvons utiliser la femme pour découvrir étions le disque est," the man in the Suburban yelled back.

I wished so desperately I had paid better attention in my high school French, but I could not understand a word he was saying.

I wanted to make them shut up, but with my mouth still gagged I was only able to communicate with my hands which of course were also bound.

Raising my gun, I tired to signal him that if he did not shut up I would kill him. But he had no idea what I was trying to tell him. And even though I was brandishing a gun with which I had already shot him in the ankle, he had no fear of me. He just looked at me the way people look at a child throwing a fit in the grocery store and kept talking back and forth in French with the guy in the Suburban.

His calm demeanor rattled me and I had to stop myself again from killing him.

Turning back to face the Suburban, I tried to peek at what he was doing. Suzanna was still nowhere in sight and he just sat there peeking over the dashboard looking back at me. Then suddenly he raised his gun and fired. Missing badly, he hit the car in the rear and I thought for a second that he did not know where I was. I turned around to check on my friend, who had turned over and started crawling for his gun again. No, not his gun, he was crawling away from the car.

It was almost too late, when I realized what he was doing. I dove away from the car just as it exploded. The concussion of the explosion threw me even further from the car and separated me from my gun. I landed on the front lawn of a nearby house. My ears were ringing and for a few seconds I was not sure what was going on around me. The first thing I realized was that I needed my gun. Crawling on my hands and knees I searched for it through the smoke and heat, but could not find it. Looking up, I could see the Suburban moving around the burning car in my direction.

Still confused from the explosion I flailed around searching for the gun. Realizing I needed cover worse than I needed the gun I scrambled to my feet and ran toward the house, diving around its corner as soon as I could. I was maybe ten yards from the house. The Suburban drove beside the man I had shot in the ankle who managed to lift himself into the vehicle while the driver pulled the man I had kicked unconscious in as well. When he was in, it turned on to the lawn and started driving toward me. I had no gun—or anything for that matter—to defend myself, but I knew both men were seriously wounded in the leg and would never be able to pursue me outside of the Suburban. So I ran.

I ran for the wooded area behind the subdivision where I knew the Suburban could not follow. I had at least fifty yards to cover. With or without shoes I never have been exceptionally fast but, when properly motivated, I can pick 'em up and put 'em down as good as the next guy. And I was motivated.

I still had about twenty yards to go when the Suburban made the corner around the house. A few steps more and the lawn ran out and I was running in my sock feet over rocks, twigs, and loose dirt. I could hear bullets whizzing past me and into the woods ahead of me. There were only a few yards more. The sirens were almost upon us.

I was close enough to dive behind the cover of a fallen pine tree when I stumbled and fell face first into the clay and rocks. The Suburban was close now. Trying to get back to my feet I collapsed under a searing pain in my right leg, which was suddenly completely limp. Using my hands I tried to make the leg work. I noticed an inordinate amount of blood on my hand. Using my left leg I forced myself from the ground, I dove over the log and into the cover of a kudzu bush.

The bullets continued for a few seconds to smash through the leaves and trees around me. I lay as close as possible to the fallen log, knowing I could ride out the storm there.

The sirens were close now and the men could not afford to hang around any longer. Spewing a stream of rock and gravel in my direction, they left the scene.

I wanted just to lie there and rest, but the police would soon be on the scene and I would be found. I thought seriously about letting them find me or even turning myself in. I had the disk now and it was decrypted. Theoretically, that was all I needed to clear my name. But I did not trust Cummings. And negotiating from jail with a piece of evidence that would probably be in an evidence room somewhere out of my control was not the position I wanted to be in.

I had to move but my leg was throbbing and burning with pain—it felt paralyzed. Crawling on my side and onto my good hip I managed to find a stick straight and sturdy enough to use as a crutch. Pulling myself to my feet, I started limping as fast as I could deeper and deeper into the woods, away from the noise of the sirens.

I hobbled back into the woods a few hundred yards. As best I could tell I was not being followed, so I collapsed behind a large, mossy limestone rock. My leg was weak and I was shaking all over from shock and exhaustion. I racked my brain for a plan, but could not focus. Confusion rolled over me like a fog. I remember sweating profusely; my shirt was drenched with it. It ran from my hair into my unbandaged eye. The trees around me started slowly, but then picked up speed, spinning around me. I closed my eyes, hoping the spinning would stop. When I opened them again everything was a whirling blur. Gradually from the corners of my vision, a darkness began to gather around me. I fought against it as best I could, but I had soon lost all power to resist it. Finally I succumbed and slipped away.

Chapter Seventeen

It was the cold. That's what woke me. Not that the weather was cold. I was cold. I had passed out drenched in sweat and when the cool evening breezes of October began to blow it made me cold.

When I came to myself, I feared that I had passed out from a loss of blood. I tried to sit-up but the pain that shot up and down my leg and back was paralyzing. My jaw was also in intense pain caused by the duct tape gag that had been tightly wrapped around my head for at least eight hours. My wrists were swollen around the tape which still bound them and smeared with dried blood. And I was afraid that my loss of consciousness had been caused by a loss of blood. But before I could check my leg I had to get this tape off my wrist and to do that I had to move my leg. Starting slowly I scooted on my side along the ground looking for a rock sharp enough to cut the tape from my wrists. With every slight change in my position my leg throbbed with pain. A few feet away I found a relatively sharp rock and began working on the tape. It took longer that expected but finally I freed my hands from the tape. It was such a relief—I could feel the blood rushing into my stiff cold figures as I rubbed them and my wrists. The tape had cut deep wounds into my wrists which were red and swollen.

151

The moment my fingers were nimble enough, I began working on the tape around my head. Again it was a relief to be able to open and close my jaw.

Using the rock I had been sleeping against I pulled myself to a standing position and looked at my leg. My pants were soaked with blood, but it did not look like so much blood that I was in some immediate danger. That was a huge relief.

To get a decent look at my leg, I had to pull my pants down. Unsnapping them I began slowly to pull them past the wound. Carefully I pulled the pant leg away from my leg. Even though the blood was not completely dry, it was fiercely painful. Finally I got the pants past the wound and I let them drop to my ankles. It was difficult to see much in the light of dusk, but what I found was an entry wound about four inches below my right hip and a corresponding exit wound in the front of my leg. The bleeding for the most part had stopped.

It looked as though I would live, at least a little longer, and therefore I needed a plan. The situation: I was in the woods with a serious bullet wound in my leg. I could not call the police because I would be arrested for a murder I did not commit. I could not go to a hospital because they are required by law to report to the police any gunshot wounds they treat. I did not have a car. I had no way of getting a car (by now either the boys from the DGSE and/or the police have staked out Paul's house hoping I would be stupid enough to return). I did not have a change of clothes. All I had was the envelope containing the disk and the print out, eighteen dollars in cash, and a makeshift walking stick.

Luckily all I had to do was find my way to a pay phone and give Cummings a call and in a matter of a few hours this whole thing would be over.

I would have him come meet me somewhere close and exchange the information. Then have Willie call the FBI and arrange for them to meet me at the hospital and this whole thing would be over.

But then there was Suzanna. I tried not to think about her. I tried hard. But I could not put her out of my mind, where she had deserved to be. I don't know what her motivation had been—probably money—but she and Paul had had a plan for that disk. And she had been willing to let me die, or worse kill me to get it. So why should I worry about her now? She had been double-dealing with me; now she was getting what she deserved. Whether she had realized it or not, she had played a high-stakes game and lost. That was her choice, not mine.

If there was a way out of her situation, she would have to figure it out by herself. It was no longer my concern.

There was only one problem with my plan—Stansfield Tanner. I could not get the image of his tortured body out of my mind. His cold hollow eyes starring blankly into nothing. The dried tears on his check. I will admit that I tried every way I knew, but I could not force it from my mind. Even the pain of hobbling out of those woods with a bullet hole in one leg and on shredded feet could not force those images from my mind. With every step they confronted me until I had to acknowledge the question I did not want to face.

Could I allow someone—anyone—to face Stan's fate while it was in my power to stop it? And the frustrating, maddening, infuriating answer was no. I couldn't. I couldn't make myself do it.

I denied it for as long as I could but as I reached the edge of the woods I realized that I would have to do something to help Suzanna.

Chapter Eighteen

It was well after dark when I limped out of the woods not far from a small Jr. Store and gas station. I needed a place to clean up, but I only had eighteen dollars in cash on me. Of course I did have friends in Atlanta, but the only people I knew good enough to show up on their doorstep in my current condition were all policemen. I knew it wouldn't be right to put them in a position like that. So I needed another plan.

I pulled the manila envelope containing the decrypted disk out from my belt and removed the list that Paul had printed in his office. On it were several hundred names, each one with a corresponding company name, job title, and city. The companies were spread all over the U.S., even a few in Canada and read like the Fortune 500 list. Job titles ranged from board members to janitor.

I searched through the list to find the names of people located in and around Atlanta. There were only three, one of which was the employee of TaraTech that Cummings had already told me about. The next guy was a Harrison Seppi, the CFO of one of the few companies on the list I did not recognize.

Using a pay phone phonebook, I looked up his name and tore the page out. I fished a quarter from my pocket and called a cab to pick me up.

About ten minutes later when night had completely settled in, the cab arrived. Leaving the stick I had used as a crutch beside the road, I limped over to the cab and with more than a little difficulty I managed to bend my leg enough to get it in the backseat.

"You all right, man?" the cabby said after watching me get in the car.

"Yeah, I was in a little accident," I said and gave him the address. "You got the time?" I said as he pulled away from the curb.

"Quarter after six."

At few minutes after 6:30 I gave the cabby sixteen dollars and struggled out of his cab in front of Harrison Seppi's house. It was a sprawling rambler spread out over a huge lawn. I limped up the long asphalt drive to the front door and rang the bell, but got no answer. The house was dark and I was sure that no one was home. I hoped Seppi was just late coming home and not out of town. I thought about breaking into the house and waiting, but I decided that the house was more than likely protected by a security alarm and that it would be better just to wait for him outside.

Finding a place in the shadows behind a large azalea bush near the garage, I waited. I tried to find a comfortable place to lay down where I could also keep an eye on the driveway. But nothing I tried offered any relief to my leg or back. One nice thing I did realize about the bullet hole through my leg was that it hurt so bad that I had almost completely forgotten about my eye.

I scrummed around in the bushes in front of Seppi's house for at least an hour before a car pulled into the driveway and the garage door opened. A man I assumed to be Seppi drove into the garage in what appeared to be a brand new Lexus. He drove past me without even a sideways glance trying to keep up with Luciano Pavorotti whose voice was teeming out of the car sound system. After parking, he got out of his car with a suit coat over his arm and a briefcase in his hand. He looked to be in his late fifties, with silver hair combed straight back. Without using a key he walked into his house, pushing the button to lower the garage door as he did. Once he was in, I ducked under the closing garage door.

I searched the garage for a weapon, but the best I could come up with was a standard-head screwdriver which had been left on a little-used workbench. In addition to the car Seppi had driven, there was another car parked in the two-car garage. Its hood was cold, indicating that hadn't been used recently. Seppi, I believed, was the only one in the house. Finally, something was breaking my way.

Opening the door to the house silently, I slipped into a small mud room and closed the door behind me. Although I could not see him, I could hear Seppi rummaging around the kitchen. Quietly, painfully I limped toward the kitchen.

I stopped at the kitchen door and listened. I could hear Seppi searching through the refrigerator. Cautiously, I peaked around the corner. There he was, bent down into his refrigerator. Only two quick steps away. Trouble was, I wasn't capable of taking even one quick step.

Of course I did have the element of surprise on my side. So I decided to risk it. I had only began hobbling into the kitchen when I startled him dropping a jar of pickles on the floor. In one quick move, he turned to face me. Simple shock turned to terror when he saw me. We both froze for a split second staring at each other. The color drained from his face. He turned to run for a phone only a few steps away sitting on a small built-in desk.

I lunged for him, but there was no spring at all in my legs and only managed to get his left foot. But I held on to in it for all I was worth. He began kicking me with his right foot, bringing his hard-soled shoe down again and again on my head, back, and arms. Reaching up, I grabbed his belt and tripped him. He flailed wildly trying to resist, but he abruptly stopped offering any resistance when I brought the screwdriver to the soft fleshy skin under his jaw.

"How are we this evening, Mr. Honorary Correspondent?" I said as I lay on top of him.

I cannot describe the look that came over his face at the mention of Honorary Correspondent. It wasn't fear. It wasn't relief. It wasn't anger. It wasn't resignation. It was all of them.

"Who . . . I . . . what . . ." he sputtered.

"You knew I would come one day, didn't you, Harry?" I said.

"Who are you?" he said.

"Someone who knows that you've been a bad boy, Monsieur Seppi," I said, mocking him in a poorly rendered French accent.

"Are you here to kill me?" he said.

"I haven't decided that yet," I said.

"Please, I'll do anything, but—" I shut him up by jamming my screwdriver harder into his jaw.

"Shut up, Seppi. The first thing you need to know is I hate you. I don't care whether you live or die tonight. In fact, I would take some pleasure in killing you with this screwdriver. So if you want to see the dawn, you will speak only when spoken to and you will do exactly as I say. Is that absolutely clear?"

He nodded his head to indicate that it was.

"Now is the time to say if it's not. Because from here on out one false move, one unrequested remark and I'm going to jam this screwdriver up through the top of your head," I said, pushing the screwdriver even harder into his jaw.

"I . . . understand," he said meekly.

"Very good, Monsieur. Now for the first question, is there a gun in this house?"

He froze, unsure how to respond, his eyes brimming with terror.

"I can see that you have one, so take me to it," I said, and made my best effort at getting off the floor without showing him how injured I was. Holding him by one arm and with the screwdriver poised at the base of his skull, I let him lead me to the gun.

We walked through the house almost to its rear and into a bedroom. Once in the bedroom he walked over to a night-stand and opened a drawer. In the drawer was a nickel-plated .45. He reached in to retrieve it. I rammed the screwdriver against his head, pushing his head so far forward that his chin was firmly planted on his chest.

"That right there is the kind of thing that is going to get you killed tonight. Did I ask you to touch the gun?" I said.

"No."

"Then don't touch it," I said as I drove the hardest punch I could into his kidney. He dropped to his knees and doubled over in pain. As he did I removed the gun from the drawer and checked to see if it was loaded.

"Don't you know you should keep the safety on?" I said.

He made no reply but sat on his knees awaiting his next order.

Also in the drawer was a box of ammunition with only nine rounds missing.

"You ever fired this thing?" I said.

"No."

"Wouldn't it be ironic if the first time this gun was fired was to put a hole in your head?" I said and made myself chuckle.

"It would indeed," Seppi said as he started to cry. It was a pathetic sight really, him on his knees crying, but I just let him do it. I needed him to be absolutely terrified of me. We had a lot to do.

"What time can we expect Mrs. Seppi tonight?" I said as I intently studied the gun.

Jerking his head up he looked at me and for a moment I could see the pure unfiltered mixture of hatred and terror in his eyes.

"She is out of town."

I began to look around the room for something to tie his hands with. Nothing was immediately visible.

"You got a pair of handcuffs in this house?" I asked almost as a joke.

He involuntarily glanced at his wife's bedside table.

"You're not much of a poker player are you, Seppi?" I said and walked around the bed to open the nightstand drawer. There sitting on the top of a collection of other knickknacks was a pair of stainless steel handcuffs with the key in the lock.

"This is a pretty good pair of cuffs," I said restraining the urge to make even more jokes. Seppi had no reaction; he just sat there on his knees, staring at the floor in front of him.

"Okay, Seppi, I need an overcoat. A long overcoat," I said.

"There's one in the closet," he said, pointing one of three doors in the bedroom. I was surprised at how easily I had subdued this "international spy."

He stayed on his knees as I backed into the closet. Seppi was an inch or two taller than I and maybe thirty pounds heavier, so I knew his coat would fit.

A moment later I walked out with a dark tan wool coat. I put the coat on. It hung halfway down my shins and was slightly too big, which was just the way I wanted it.

"What size shoes do you wear?" I asked.

"Ten, ten and a half," he said.

"Got any nine and a half?"

"No, I don't think so."

I grabbed a pair of tennis shoes from the nearest shelf.

"Any socks?" I yelled from the closet.

"Top drawer," he said, looking at the tattered and bloody pair I was wearing.

I opened the drawer and produced a new pair of athletic socks with the tags and stickers still affixed.

"Okay, Seppi, I need to get cleaned up," I said as I took the coat off and laid it on the bed. Then grabbing him by the arm we walked into the bathroom closet. Then, making him kneel and reach around either side of the toilet bowl, I handcuffed his hands through the narrow space between the toilet's base and the wall.

"Just sit here and keep your mouth shut while I clean up a bit," I said through the door.

The bathroom was large, with several full-length mirrors. It was the first time I had looked at myself in several days. I decided that people were being kind when they said how bad I looked.

In addition to my clothes being tattered and torn, the bandage around my head and eye, which was not yet twenty-four hours old, was filthy with sweat, blood, dirt, and clay. The part of my face that was visible was cut and scratched, the stitches were red and swollen, I hadn't shaved in several days, and a deep dark circle had formed under my good eye.

Sitting on the edge of an oversized bathtub I carefully removed my socks. My feet were cut and bruised all over. Using my fingernails and a pair of tweezers I had found in one of the drawers, I removed as many of the thorns, stickers, and tiny pebbles as I could. Then spinning on my rear end, I put my feet into the bathtub and let the warm water run over them. It felt so good I didn't want to stop, but I knew I did not have time to waste. Using a bar of soap, I washed my feet and rinsed them one more time.

Next, I turned my attention to my face. I found a clean towel and wash cloth and tried to clean good enough that I could go into a store without drawing to much attention to myself. My arms and wrists looked as bad as my face, but the swelling in my wrist and fingers was already going down.

I washed my face and hands and combed my hair. I walked back into the bedroom, put on the socks, shoes, and overcoat, putting Seppi's gun in one pocket and the box of ammunition in the other. Then walking back to the bathroom, I uncuffed Seppi, brought him back into the bedroom, and sat him on the bed. I took a seat on an upholstered chair in the corner of the room.

"Okay, Seppi, how do you contact the DGSE?" I said.

I could tell he considered, at least for a second, professing ignorance.

"Watch it," I said, removing the gun from my pocket.

"They contact me. When they need me," he said, looking away from me.

"Then what?"

"I get what they want and we meet somewhere."

"Where?"

"Changes every time. They don't call that often."

"Now, Seppi, you're not trying to tell me you have no way of contacting these people, are you?" I said.

"I have a number to call but I've never used it," he said.

"There's a first time for everything. Where is the number?"

"I have it committed to memory," he said, pointing to his head.

"Good. Get them on the phone."

"My instructions are to never call them from my home or—"

"Get them on the phone now," I said, rising from my chair with some difficulty.

He quickly jumped around the bed, picked up the phone, and started dialing. I made him hold the phone so that I could hear.

The phone was answered in the middle of its second ring.

"Hello," an older man's voice said.

"I need a pickup," Seppi said.

"You are not scheduled for some time. Is it urgent?"

"Yes, I'm afraid it is."

"I need your request, then."

" 'Ask not for whom the bell tolls, it tolls for thee,' " Seppi said.

"Is Hemingway your favorite?"

"No, I prefer Victor Hugo."

"Okay," the man said after he and Seppi had gotten past the code words. "Is this phone secure?"

I grabbed the phone from his hand before he could answer.

"This is Lafayette Henrie. Do you recognize that name?"

There was a silence on the other end.

"Please hold," he said.

A second later a younger woman picked up the phone.

"To whom am I speaking?" she said with a heavy French accent.

"This is Lafayette Henrie. Do you know who I am?"

"Yes, yes, I do, Mr. Henrie. How—"

"Shut up and listen. I've got your disk. And I want to talk to someone who can make a deal."

"There is no one here authorized to make such a deal," she said.

"Here is what you need to do if you want to keep this disk from the CIA and Mr. Seppi here alive. In one hour I want to talk to Ms. Tanner. If she is alive and unharmed I'll talk to someone about a deal."

"I understand," the woman said.

"I'm calling in one hour. If you're not ready, Mr. Seppi is dead. Then I'll find another of your Honorary Correspondents and we'll try again. Am I understood?"

"Yes, Mr. Henrie, you are," she said, and I hung up.

"Now, Seppi, you need your wallet and car keys. We're going for a little ride."

Seppi got his car keys and a coat. I cuffed his hands behind him and put him in the passenger seat.

I had Seppi direct me to a drugstore not far from his house. I pulled into the parking lot and parked as close as I could to the door.

"Here's the plan. We're going in here and buy a few things. I'm going to uncuff you and keep this gun in my pocket, but believe me I won't think twice about dropping you in that store. I'll leave your dead body in there and go to the next Correspondent on the list. Got it?"

"Yes," he said.

"Okay, let's go," I said.

We both got out of the car and walked through the automatic doors. I grabbed a shopping basket and put it in his hands.

"Lighten up a bit," I said with a little chuckle.

He made no response but followed me around the store like a three-year-old following his mother.

I picked up a several of bottles of peroxide, a large bag of cotton balls, a stack of sterile bandages, five rolls of sterile gauze, several Ace bandages, and some toiletries. Once I had everything I needed we went to the checkout line and Seppi dutifully paid the tab.

After getting back into the car, I handcuffed him again and made the ten-minute drive to the Cumberland Mall just off I 285 southeast of Marietta. By the car's clock I still had thirty-five minutes before I was scheduled to make the call.

Again I parked near the door.

"This time I need some new clothes," I said as I uncuffed him.

"Okay," was the sum of his response.

Walking into the front door I found the first men's clothing store I could find and picked out a shirt and a pair of slacks.

Again Seppi paid without being asked. By Seppi's watch

we had only five minutes. I asked the store clerk where to find some pay phones. He directed me across the mall to the food court.

My leg was hurting so bad I could no longer put very much weight on it. I put my arm around Seppi's neck, who didn't offer any protest to essentially carrying me across the mall to the phones.

After leaning me against the wall, he dialed the number.

"Hello," said the woman from the earlier call.

"I need a pickup," Seppi said.

"You are not scheduled for some time. Is it urgent?"

"Yes, I am afraid it is."

"I need your request, then."

" 'Ask not for whom the bell tolls, it tolls for thee,' " Seppi said.

"Is Hemingway your favorite?"

"No, I prefer Victor Hugo."

"Put Mr. Henrie on the line," she said.

"Put Suzanna on," I said before she could speak.

"Hold please," she said.

"Hank. Hank, are you there?" said a distraught Suzanna.

"Are you okay, Suzanna?" I said as though I might not like it if she were.

"No—well, I'm alive if that's what you mean," she said and broke down in tears.

"Your girlfriend? She is unharmed, Mr. Henrie. We can make a deal, no?" said the woman I had spoken to before.

"Yes, we can make a deal. It's just after nine o'clock. Let's meet at eleven P.M. I'll call you about a quarter till eleven to let you know where," I said.

"Why so long, Mr. Henrie?" she said, more than a little suspicious.

" 'Cause one of your goons has shot me and I've got to take care of that first," I said.

"Eleven would be fine, Mr. Henrie. But I think it only— what is the word—sporting . . . no, fair. It is only fair to warn you—if I have even the slightest provocation, Mrs. Tanner will die like her former husband. You understand me, no?" she said.

I thought for a second about threatening Seppi's life, but realized they cared nothing for him and knowing that he was compromised, they would probably like it if I killed him.

"Yes, I understand. And that of course makes it very easy for me to give the CIA what they want and save my own hide in the process. You understand me, no?"

"Yes, Mr. Henrie, I believe we understand each other," she said, her voice tinged with anxiety.

It was a good sign as far as I was concerned.

I was moving forward as though I had a plan because it was the only way I could keep Suzanna alive. But I didn't have a plan and I could feel panic begin to set in. I was finding it hard to concentrate on the problem at hand because of the pain in my back, leg and eye. I had the decrypted disk. The challenge was to use the disk to gain Suzanna's release without actually giving up the disk so that I could turn around and trade the disk for the information of Stan's killers. There was no time to put together an elaborate plan, I was making it up as I went.

My next move was to have Seppi check us into a hotel. He had several hundred dollars in cash so I made him use it instead of a credit card.

Once in the room I handcuffed Seppi to the lamp which was securely bolted to a stud behind the wall. Then I unplugged the phone and took it with all of the rest of the things I had purchased into the bathroom.

First, I carefully removed the filthy eye bandage and examined my eye in the mirror. It looked worse than it felt, if that was possible. Using some of the cotton swabs and peroxide I cleaned around my eye and stitches as best I could.

Satisfied that I had cleaned them as well as I could, I

drew a very hot bath and slowly slipped in. The area around the gunshot wound was bright red, swollen and hot to the touch. The hot water stung at first, but gradually the leg began to ease as the water released the pressure which had been building in the leg. I sat in the tub longer than I should have, letting my leg and back soak. Finally I drained the water and took a hot shower.

As the pain in my leg began to ease I could concentrate on a plan. Even though I knew I had to help Suzanna if I could, I indulged myself by pretending to argue back and forth about what I should do. I mean what was I really going to do if it came down to saving Suzanna or the disk. But soon I realized I was wasting valuable time and put those thoughts completely out of my mind.

As I considered what I was up against, I realized I needed some way to level the playing field. The only way to save Suzanna and keep the disk was to double cross the French somehow.

My first problem was to get Suzanna out safely. I puzzled for a long time over that that one. How could I be sure she was safely out of their grasp. Even though I would try to force their hand I was sure they would not willingly let her walk away if they were confident of getting the disk. Their preference was to have us both dead. So obviously I could not show up disk in hand—that would be suicide. If the disk was at some other location then at least I would have a little negotiating leverage. It wouldn't be much, but it would be something at least.

Gradually a plan began to form. There were no good options, so I was left to choose the best of a lot of bad options.

I accredited myself only one advantage—the ability to stay calm under pressure and think on my feet. There are a lot of people who can outwork me, and there are a lot of people tougher than me. And I had never really been accused of out-hustling very many people. But one thing I have always been confident of is my ability to outthink my opponent. Of course there are plenty who would even question that as one of my strengths, but I knew that when I had to do it, I could outthink just about anybody. But to really focus my mind, I had to be a little panicked. And I was now a little panicked.

Chapter Nineteen

I must have sat in the shower for an hour roughing out a plan. Nothing seemed to fit together until I thought of the Atlanta Hartsfield Airport. I was never going to completely level the playing field, but the airport would come as close as possible. Airports are unique in that they are easily accessible, but still very secure. What I liked most about my idea was that it was next to impossible to sneak a weapon into an airport especially on short notice.

After the shower I rebandaged my leg and eye, then dressed in my new clothes. I didn't feel real good about it, but I had a plan. It wasn't a great plan or even a good plan, but it was the best I could do with what I had to work with.

One thing I did feel good about was after having been away from police work for well over two years, I could finally feel myself thinking like a cop again. The key to my success when I was on the Atlanta PD had been leaving options open. Many people looked at solving crimes like assembling the pieces of a jigsaw puzzle. It is a useful analogy, but not completely accurate. To me, solving a crime is more like assembling a jigsaw puzzle, whose pieces can and often do change shapes.

What I found most useful in figuring out "whodunit" was keeping an open mind. When I walked on to a crime scene,

I knew only one thing for certain and that was that I did not commit the crime. Other than that fact, I tried to keep my mind open to any other possibility. Even when a piece of evidence would seem to foreclose a certain avenue, I forced myself to keep my mind open to the possibility that I had misread some bit of evidence—that I might be missing something important. Even then I often over looked or misread important pieces of evidence. So I learned that if I focused in too quickly on one theory of the crime that important clues would pass unnoticed right under my nose.

I went all the way back to the beginning and rethought everything that had happened since the morning Suzanna had awakened me. If I had been thinking like this way back then, clearly I would have began suspecting Suzanna was not playing it straight with me. The hints and suggestions she came up with were obviously more than good guesses or off-the-top-of-the-head suggestions. The most obvious being that she so easily figured out that these guys were after something in Stan's safe-deposit box. How I had just accepted that without even questioning her was perhaps the biggest mistake I had made in this whole mess. Had I been thinking properly, her leaps of logic—though they were small—would have raised all sorts of red flags.

I dwelt on all my mistakes for a few more minutes before deciding to write the whole thing off to rustiness and being caught off guard. But I knew my next mistake might well be fatal. So there could be no more.

I found Seppi where I had left him. He was a pathetic sight, handcuffed to the lamp. The few hours he had spent with me had added ten years to his face. His hair, which had been silver and perfectly combed into place, when I meet him, was now gray and hanging in frazzled strands across his forehead. Deep, dark circles had formed around his eyes. His mouth, drawn and tight, hung slightly. He was so despondent that he barely took notice of me walking out of the bathroom.

"Seppi, you can relax. This is almost over," I said.

He responded with an almost imperceptible nod of his head, staring blankly through the floor between the two twin beds.

Sitting on the bed across from his I plugged back in the phone and called the Atlanta PD's headquarter to see who the dispatch officer was that night. Sgt. O'Malley—what do you know, another break.

Smiling for the first time since Suzanna had dropped that twenty-five grand in front of me, I uncuffed Seppi from the lamp and headed out to the car, stopping only at the concierge's desk to pick up a padded envelope and a few stamps.

Seppi was in no condition to drive, so I cuffed his hands in front of him and again sat him in the passenger seat. My first stop was the mailbox just off Martin Luther King Avenue on Butler Street. Where, in the package I had gotten from the hotel concierge, I mailed the disk to my post office box in Marianna. I hesitated for a few seconds, thinking what a big risk I was taking just dropping something so important in the US mail. But knowing I didn't have any other options, I took a deep breath and dropped it in.

Twenty minutes later, I drove into the short-term parking at the Atlanta Hartsfied Airport. I parked the car and removed the handcuffs from Seppi's hands.

"Listen to me," I said, holding both his hands and trying to engage his eyes, "This is almost over. All I need you to do now is buy three plane tickets, one for a friend of mine, one for me, and one for yourself. Then make a phone call for me and you're done."

"This isn't going to be over for me anytime soon," he said, looking at me for the first time since we left the mall. "Unless I'm dead," he added as an afterthought.

"Look, Harry—that is what you go by, isn't it?"

"Harrison actually," he said, and the dullness returned to his eyes.

"Okay, Harrison. The best thing you can do when I get done with you is get on a plane to Washington, find a lawyer, and try to cut a deal with the FBI," I said.

"I don't think the FBI can protect me," he said.

"They can certainly do better than you could on your own. But then again I don't really care. Let's go," I said as I got out of the car and put his cellular phone into my pocket.

Once inside the airport, we found a pay phone and dialed Willie's home number. He answered on the fourth ring.

"Hello."

"Willie, are you coming to choir practice, you're late," Seppi said just as I had coached him.

There was a moment's hesitation before Willie said, "I . . . yeah, I almost forgot. I'll be there in about ten or fifteen minutes. Thanks."

"Good-bye," said Seppi and I hung up the phone.

Next we found a Delta ticketing counter and I had Seppi use his credit card to buy a seat on a flight to Tampa that stopped over in Tallahassee. They checked his ID and marked the ticket for boarding. This was the ticket I was going to use for Suzanna.

We then found a United ticketing counter. I didn't think I would need it, but just in case I had Seppi buy a ticket for me on a later flight to Tallahassee. It is nice to have options.

After United we went to the Continental counter.

"Go wherever you want, but be gone from here in thirty minutes," I said to him as we approached the ticketing agent.

"What time is you next flight to Washington, D.C.?" he asked, apparently having decided to take my advice.

"Let me check," the man behind the counter said. "Yes, it's wheels-up in fifteen minutes."

"Can I make it?" Seppi said.

"If we hurry."

Five minutes later Seppi and I were running to the gate. We made it with only a few minutes to spare.

"Okay Harrison," I said as he was about to board. "Just get on the plane, take your seat, and sit quietly until you land. After that I don't care. The only reason I'm letting you go is that I think you're smart enough to understand that the further you get from this airport the safer you are. Don't make me regret this."

"I won't," he said.

I released his arm and he boarded the plane.

Finding the nearest pay phone, I called the Poplar Hill Baptist Church.

"Hello," Willie said.

"Good, you're there," I said.

"You're lucky, too. I don't have a key to this place. I had to break in. Anyway, what's going on?" he said.

"It's a long story that I don't have time to go into now. I'm putting Suzanna on a flight to Tampa that stops over in Tallahassee in about an hour. I need you to be in Tallahassee with the police to pick her up."

"The police?"

"Yeah, it's the only place she's going to be safe until I can finish sorting this thing out."

"Why don't you just have her picked up in Mobile?"

"I'm back in Atlanta and it is a long story. Just trust me."

"Okay."

"Good, now listen to me very carefully Willie. I need you to take your pager with you. When I am ready I'm going to page you with four ones. When you get that message I want you to call Sgt. O'Malley with Atlanta PD and tell him that the mailbox right outside the station on Butler Street is about to be robbed and to arrest the guys who are doing it."

"Got it. What do I do if I don't get paged?" he asked.

"Don't call him. That will mean something has gone wrong and it will be better for me if they don't get arrested."

"Well, if you're going to page me, why don't you just call O'Malley yourself when you get ready?"

"I will if I can. But these guys are not going to let me out of their sight, so I'm going to take a mobile phone and page you without taking the phone out of my pocket. Once I page you I'll just turn myself into Airport Security."

"Airport Security?"

"Yeah that's where it'll be going down."

"Why the airport?"

"No guns. They won't be able to bring their guns in here,"

"And if they take you with them to the mailbox, you'll just get arrested along with them."

"Right. Either way, they're in jail and the disk is safe. But if something goes wrong or I screw it up some how, I need to be able to let them have the disk. That is why you have to wait for my page," I said, liking my plan more and more.

"Okay, I get it. So you page me with a 1111 message and I call O'Malley. Other than that, I just make sure Suzanna gets into police custody."

"What if you need me to call O'Malley, but can't page me for some reason?" he asked, easily spotting the holes in my plan.

"I'm gonna have to take some risks, and that's one of them," I said.

"Just don't get yourself killed. We can work around anything else. Never been very good at raising people from the dead," Willie said.

"Worse comes to worst, I'm going to just let them have the disk and take my chances in court."

"Yeah, but these guys are going to want the disk, and

you . . . well, you know . . . these guys are cold-blooded killers."

"Just do what I've asked you and I think everything will be fine."

"I'll be at the airport and waiting on your page."

"Thanks, Willie."

With everything in place, I looked at my watch. It was 10:45—time to make the call.

"Hello," said the same woman who I had spoken with a couple of hours before.

"This is Henrie," I said, pronouncing my name with a phony French accent, making it sound more like "ornery" than Henrie.

"Yes, Mr. Henrie, you are ready to make a trade, no?"

"Meet me at the airport in fifteen minutes just outside of gate C43. Bring Suzanna. No Suzanna—no disk. I'll be waiting," I said.

"Mr. Henrie, you must take me for some kind of idiot. I have no intention of meeting you at the airport," she said. Unlike Seppi she was probably a great poker player.

"It makes very little difference to me if you come or not. I can't believe I'm doing this anyway. Ms. Tanner and her friend have already tried to kill me today. This is my first, last, and only offer. Come to the airport and get your disk."

"Please hold," she said.

I was on hold for only a few seconds before she came back on the line and said, "We will arrive in fifteen minutes. Be there with the disk, Mr. Henrie."

Five minutes later I was sitting by the appointed gate waiting. As I did I wrote a note to include with Suzanna's ticket:

Suzanna,
    This is a direct flight to Tampa, however it stops in Tallahassee to pick up more passengers. Get off in

Tallahassee. W F will meet you there and see that you are safely cared for until this whole thing is over.

Hank

After I had written the note and tucked it into Suzanna's ticket envelope, I entered Willie's pager number into Seppi's cellular phone so that all I would have to do, when the time came, would be to press SEND. Once that was done, all I had to do was wait. As I did, I studied the people around me. They were the normal collection of people you expect to find in an airport—business travelers with suit bags on wheels, exhausted vacationers returning home and excited relatives awaiting the return of a long parted family member. I was relieved that everyone around me seemed unconcerned with me and what I might be up to.

The next ten minutes passed like minutes in a dentist's chair. But finally I spotted them as they rounded the corner from the escalator toward gate C43. There were two men on either side of Suzanna each with a firm grip on one of her arms and a smartly dressed woman in her forties walking purposefully in front. Suzanna was clearly scared and had a bruise directly under her left eye, but other than that she appeared to be fine.

As they approached I stood.

"Good evening, Mr. Henrie. You are looking . . . well," said the woman, with a mocking grin on her face. She had short dark hair, an equally dark complexion and stood at least two inches taller than me. Under different circumstances I was sure I would have found her very attractive.

"Thank you, I work out regularly," I said.

"I have Ms. Tanner," she said, gesturing over her shoulder. "Where is my disk?"

"I have a plane ticket for Ms. Tanner." I held it up for her to see. "When she is safely aboard the plane and it has taken off you can have your disk. Not before."

"Then you have wasted my time, Mr. Henrie," she said, with her hands on her hips and contempt in her eyes.

"Fine," I said, throwing up my hands as if I didn't care. Then looking at Suzanna I said, "I've done what I could and considering what you tried to do to me today. I think it is more than you could expect." I must admit, even though it probably belies a character flaw, I enjoyed the look on Suzanna's face as she heard what I had said.

She completely broke down, crying uncontrollably.

"Fine, Mr. Henrie, you may have it your way. I will let her go and you can become my collateral," she said, and nodded to her goons as a way of telling them to release Suzanna.

I handed the ticket to Suzanna as she approached me.

"You are on the flight to Tampa that leaves from this gate in five minutes," I said.

As I handed her the ticket and she took the first steps away from her captors a look of elation swept over her face. "Thank you," she said under her breath, but with a contrite glance into my eyes. I made no reply, but simply watched as she boarded the plane.

"She is gone, Mr. Henrie. Where is my disk?" the tall woman said, becoming increasingly impatient.

"Not until the plane has taken off," I said, letting them know I also meant business.

A few minutes later the plane backed way from the gate and taxied toward the runway.

"Now, Mr. Henrie, the disk," the woman said as the plane left our sight.

"How can I be certain you won't kill me once I give it to you?" I said stalling for time.

"Mr. Henrie, I am growing tired of these delays. Where may I find my disk?" she said, yelling the last sentence so loud it attracted the attention of those around us.

I hoped the attention would cause her to tone it down a

bit, but she was not the least bit concerned with the attention she was attracting.

One of the men, who had been holding Suzanna's arm opened his suit coat. I tried not to, but I am sure a mix of surprise and fear crossed my face when I saw what he was discreetly attempting to show me—a pistol neatly tucked into a well worn shoulder holster.

Just as I was trying to figure out how they got the gun into the airport I saw an airport policeman walking down the corridor in our direction. Unconcerned with us, he seemed to be walking his rounds, stopping to visit some of the vendors he knew and checking out the newspapers and magazines on the stands.

"This man has a gun!" I yelled to attract his attention and turned to run.

I had not made one step when the two goons tackled me from behind and began wrestling my hands behind my back. From behind me I could hear a familiar voice approaching say, "It's okay officer. FBI. This has all been cleared with your commanding officer, Captain Nelson."

Looking up as the men on my back were clamping on a pair of handcuffs and I saw Cummings flashing the same phony ID he had used on me at Blue Springs. He put his arm around the officer and gently steered him out of earshot.

"It's a fake officer. That ID is a fake. These people are spies." Even I could not believe how incredibly stupid that sounded as it came out of my mouth. The policeman just laughed and turned his attention back to Cummings. As he did, one of the men kneeling on my back delivered a sharp quick blow to my mouth, slitting both my upper and my lower lip.

Cummings and the policeman were having a conversation, but they were out of my earshot and I was unable to make out what they were saying. Meanwhile, the blood from my mouth ran down my chin and on to the floor, while one of the men held my legs so that I could not move them and the other let all his weight rest on his knee which was planted firmly in the middle of my back. It was all I could do to keep forcing breaths of air into my lungs. Speaking was out of the question.

The policeman took Cummings's ID and made a call on his hand-held radio. I presumed he was attempting to check whether it was authentic or not. Of course, it was fake, but Cummings would not have given it to him if he had not had a way making sure it would be verified as authentic. Sure enough, a minute or so later the policeman turned around and handed Cummings back his ID.

"Here's your ID, Agent Cummings. Do you need any help?" he said as they walked back toward where I was being subdued.

"No, thank you, officer, I think we have it under control," he said.

"Get him on his feet," he said to the men. "Lafayette Henrie, you are under arrest for the murder of Stansfield Tanner," he said, and finished reading my rights as the two men escorted me away.

Chapter Twenty

Ten minutes later I was sitting in the rear seat of a parked car on the top floor of short-term parking in the Atlanta Hartsfield Airport. On either side of me were the two goons who had escorted Suzanna into the airport and me out. My lips were black, blue, and swollen from the shot I had taken in the airport. The handcuffs, which were entirely too tight, were digging into my already sore wrist.

Outside the car stood Cummings talking to the dark haired French woman I had negotiated with for Suzanna's release. They both had their backs to the car and I could not hear what they were saying. I sat, somewhat squished, between the two silent goons, who stared straight forward as though I were not even there. My mind was racing. I knew I could not tell them where the disk was located because I would not be able to page Willie with my hands cuffed behind my back. I decided my best chance lay in stalling until a better opportunity presented itself.

After what seemed like five to ten minutes Cummings turned around, opened the front passenger door, sat down, and turned to face me.

"I'm trying to save your life here, Henrie, but you're going to have to help me," he said. I could feel the hate coursing through my entire body and out through my eyes.

179

The absolute frustration of the situation paralyzed me—mind and body. I just sat rigid and refused to respond.

"You ever hear of a guy by the name of Sammy Gritton? I believe he was known as 'The Grinder,' " he said as he opened up the front cover of a manila folder so that I could see a grainy photo of a middle-aged man with a bad toupee and a slight pot belly. I had heard of him before. From what little I knew he was a hitman from New Orleans who occasionally did jobs in Atlanta.

"I've heard of him, so what?" I said through gritted teeth.

"He's your man. He popped Tanner. I got everything you're going to need to hang it on him and clear yourself right here," he said, patting the folder. "But I've got to have that disk."

I could see that the folder was stuffed with important, official looking papers, but I was sure it was more of a stage prop than any kind of useful evidence linking Gritton to Stan's murder.

"Who are you, Cummings?" I said.

"Quit wasting time, Henrie. You're out of options. Give me that disk," he said, his frustration beginning to show as well.

"That disk is the only thing keeping me alive and you nor anyone else is getting it until I have some assurances," I said.

"The only reason they finally killed Tanner was they re-alized he did not know where that key was. Otherwise . . . they'd have gotten it out of him. Just like they'll get it out of you," he said, trying to engage me with eye contact.

"Even if I told them they could not get the disk without me?" I said finally.

"What do you mean?" he said.

"I mean I've got it somewhere that only I can get it." It was a little bit of a bluff, but I didn't have anything else to lose.

"Only you can get it? Only you?" he said.

"Only me."

"Well, then, with you dead, you might say the disk is in safe keeping," he said with a smile.

I wasn't quite sure how to respond.

"Look, Henrie, we both know it can be gotten to, no matter where it is. The only question now is are we going to do it the hard way or the easy way," he said.

So that was it. They were through trying to make me believe that they might let me live through this if I would only cooperate. The offer now was: we'll kill you quickly if you cooperate, otherwise . . .

"I might be scared, if this whole thing went away with me, but it doesn't, you can't kill it with me. There are other loose ends."

This brought a sincere laugh.

"Are you kidding me? That is what I do. Tie your loose ends. But the money on this one is so good, I might not even worry about tying them up. I may just disappear and let someone else worry about this mess. Don't fool yourself into thinking we're worried about any loose ends."

"Were you ever with the CIA?" I asked, trying to stall for time.

"My whole career. Still am and this is the break I've been looking for a long time."

"Break?" I said sensing that his vanity was getting the better of him.

"Yeah, you know, a deal I could make some big money on."

"So you are on the payroll of the DGSE?" I said and as I did he caught himself, realizing that he was talking too much.

"Henrie, this is not about me. Come on, do yourself a favor. Where's the disk?"

"You think these guys are going to let you live when this whole thing is over? You're going to be a liability just like me, Cummings. You do realize that, don't you?" I said.

He nodded to the goon sitting to my left who delivered an elbow to my nose and mouth, snapping my head backward so sharply it almost knocked me out. Blood dripped from my nose and the reopened wounds in my lip. I shook my head to clear the cobwebs just in time to see the elbow coming up for another shot.

Chapter Twenty-one

I woke up—I don't know how much later—in a place I did not recognize. I came to and collected my thoughts before they realized I was conscious. It wasn't much of one, but it was at least a small break for me. Sitting perfectly still I tried to assess my situation.

I had been stripped to my underwear and tied to a chair in the way Stan had been when I found him. I could not see much of the building I was in without moving my head and tipping off that I was conscious, but I appeared to be in a small warehouse or a mechanic's garage of some kind.

A plan began to form in my mind. It would have been nice if I could get them all to leave somehow, but I realized that was not likely to happen—while I was still alive, anyway. I could however, if I played it smart, get them to leave me alone with only one or two people. Just one if I was lucky.

It was, of course, easy to figure out the best was to get at least a couple of them to leave—tell them where I had hidden the disk. They would want to make sure the information I had given them was accurate before killing me and that would mean leaving to check it out.

I sat still for another minute or two, then I allowed myself a cough and shake my head as though I were coming to.

"Ah, Mr. Henrie, you have rejoined us," said the woman from the airport. As she spoke the lights of a car parked about ten yards in from of me came on, and I could hear her and her two thugs approaching me. I said nothing.

"Agent Cummings informs me that you wish to do this . . . how did he say it . . . the hard way?" She stood directly between the two car lights with her goons on either side of her. All I could see was the darkened silhouettes of their bodies.

I squinted against the light and said nothing.

"Very well, then I will give you one last chance before we begin. Where is the disk?"

Again, no response.

She nodded to her goons. The fatter of the two men walked around behind me and braced the chair from falling backward while the other man rolled up his shirtsleeves and unsheathed a long hunting knife. I had seen his handiwork with that particular instrument and wanted no part of it.

"Commencez," she said when the men appeared ready.

"Okay, I'll tell you," I said at the last possible moment.

"S'arrêtent," she said. "Quickly, Mr. Henrie. I have grown tired of you."

"It is in a mailbox on Butler Street just off MLK in a small package addressed to me," I said looking down into my lap.

"MLK?" she said.

"Martin Luther King Avenue," I explained.

Suddenly I felt the cold steel of the knife being held tightly against my throat and the man looked over for permission to cut my throat.

"Not yet," the woman said. "We must first make sure the disk is where he has said. Jean, you and Mr. Cummings will come with me. Claude, you will stay with Mr. Henrie."

"Wait a minute." I heard Cummings, who I still could not see.

"Get in the car, Cummings, and keep quiet," she said as she stamped out her half-smoked cigarette.

"But I—" Cummings began to protest.

"Now, Mr. Cummings," she said, ending any complaint from him.

Within a few moments, all three were in the car and Claude opened a large garage door to let them out. With the light out of my eyes it took a while before I could see around the room. It was smaller than I had originally thought. To my left, almost out of my sight was a small metal table with four chairs scattered around it and my clothes wadded in a ball on top. Claude had taken a seat at the table in a chair facing me and picked up a magazine to read. Other than the table and chairs there was no furniture. On the walls hung a few old chains, hoses, and pipes, but the place looked as though it had long since been abandoned.

I had no idea where in the city I was, therefore I had no idea how long it would take them to get to the mailbox. I just knew I needed to work quickly.

First, I tested my hands; they were secured tightly with handcuffs, so tight in fact that I was losing all feeling in them. My feet were a little looser than my hands, having been tied with some type of twine. As I quietly strained against the knots, the twine loosened enough that it would slide up and down the chair leg as I moved my legs.

Claude still sat at the table facing me, but not paying particularly close attention.

Using my toes I began to rock the chair back and forth. That got Claude's attention.

"Stop that," he said in heavily accented French.

But before he had got the words out of his mouth I had managed to tip the chair over on its back. I tried to lower my feet passed the bottom of the chair and slide the twine off, but I could not do it while on my back, I needed to be on my side. Claude, who was shouting something in French was out of his chair and on his way over. I rocked from side to side as best I could as he made his way over. Each rock took me closer and closer to tipping on to my side. When he was only a few feet away, I finally tipped over. I was in a better position now to move my feet, but still I could only free one foot.

Suddenly, I felt the cold steel of Claude's knife at my throat again and from the corner of my eye I could see him standing over me.

"Mr. Henrie, it is useless. You can not escape. But if you prefer, I can kill you now," he said as though he were simply asking his dog if he wanted to go for a walk.

I said nothing, but sat perfectly still. He held the knife at my throat, letting it press into my skin for another few seconds before he reached over with his other hand and began lifting the chair to a sitting position.

I decided to make one more subtle attempt to free my second leg. Just as the front leg of the chair was about to hit the floor, the rope slipped off. I quickly moved my feet into position so they would look as though they were still tied to the chair.

With the chair back on all fours, Claude reared back with his right hand bringing it with all his force into my left check almost spinning my head completely around.

"Henrie, I think we would both like it better if you just sit still," he said in very stilted English. Then he stood back to look at me. Up and down he looked, apparently finding everything to his liking, because he turned to walk back to his chair. It was then that I made my move.

As he walked away from me I reached out my right foot and tripped him. As he was falling to the ground, I sprung to my feet trying to get to his head so that I could kick him unconscious. But he was more agile than I had expected and he bounced up to his hands and knees. I reared back and kicked him as hard as I could in the ribs and although it knocked him back to the ground, I am sure it hurt me more than it hurt him. The gunshot wound from earlier in the evening throbbed and felt as though my whole leg was expanding and contracting with each beat of my heart.

Again he was on his hands and knees before I could do anything. I knew that if I let him back to his feet it was over for me and I only had a few more kicks in my leg. So I delivered another, this one even harder than the first and I could hear it take the wind out of him. Undaunted, he lifted himself again.

This time I tried a different approach. Turning my back on him, I drove the legs of my chair down into his back as hard as I could pushing him back to the floor as he screamed with pain. But when he did, he managed to reach around and knock my feet out from under me, sending me and my chair crashing to the ground at his side.

We both scrambled to our feet. His knife lay at my feet. My eyes followed his to his gun which lay on the table next to my clothes. I was at least two steps closer to the table than he. He broke for the table. I took two steps and launched myself into him, knocking us both to the ground, both of us landing with a thud, overturning the table and spilling its contents all over the cement floor.

Again I scrambled to my feet expecting to find him diving for the gun. But he must have hit his head during the fall, because he seemed to have trouble getting to his feet. I hurried over to finish what I had started and tried to deliver a kick to the bottom of his chin.

At the last possible second, however, he raised his arm blocking my foot and sending me back to the floor. But as I hit the floor I saw my opening, and without thinking I coiled my good leg and with all the strength I could muster I unleashed a kick to his mouth that snapped his head back and drove his teeth deep into my bare foot. Simultaneous with the snap of his head he collapsed unconscious face-down on the floor.

My condition was only slightly better than his, I was drenched in sweat and completely spent. The rope around my chest was tied so tight I could not catch my breath. I lay on the floor for a minute trying to gather the strength to get up and find the key to the handcuffs. I had to work quickly because I was not sure how long it was going to take them to get to the mailbox.

Finally I struggled to my feet. My legs were shaking as I walked over to where the contents of the table had spilled onto the floor. After some searching I found what looked like a set of handcuff keys. With my feet I kicked them to a clear place on the floor and lay down on them so that I could pick them up with my hands. Once they were in my hands I rolled to my side and began trying to unlock the cuffs.

It was extremely difficult because my fingers had lost most of their feeling and my wrists were so sore that every twist of my hand sent sharp pains up my arm. Each minute that passed offered that much less of a chance that I would ever catch Cummings and his friends.

Suddenly, the key slipped into place and with one quick turn my left wrist was free of the cuff. Then, with more effort than I imagined necessary, I was able to shimmy out of the rope tied around my chest and free of the chair.

Next I needed a phone. I looked through the things that had been on the table and did not find one. I crawled over to Claude and began searching his clothes, where I found a cellular phone in the breast pocket of his suit coat.

From memory I dialed the number to Sgt. O'Malley's desk.

"O'Malley," he answered.

"O'Malley, this is Hank Henrie," I said.

"Hank, you got this whole place turned upside down. Where are you?" he said.

"I'm ready to come in, but I need you to do some thing for me."

"What?" he said very incredulously.

"There are two men and a woman about to break into a mailbox right outside your office. Get somebody out there to arrest them."

"Do what?"

"O'Malley, you're wasting time. Get someone out there right now." I said, trying to invoke some urgency.

"You're kidding, right?" he said.

"No, I am not kidding," I said, holding the phone in front of my face and yelling into it.

"All right, calm down. I'll do it, I'll have to bring you in, too, though. Hang on," he said. I could hear his hand muffling the phone as he yelled out some orders.

Then, out of the corner of my eye I could see the shadow of something being swung at me.

Dropping the phone to the floor I ducked and tried to roll, as some kind of metal bar came crushing down on my back knocking me to the floor. Without thinking I rolled on to my back twice and narrowly missed the second blow of the pipe.

Sometime, without me noticing it, Claude had come to. I tried to get to my feet but another bone-crushing blow to my back sent me to the floor again. I could hear his heavy breathing behind me as I attempted to get up from the floor. There was a sharp, fierce pain in my side that caused my arm to collapse under me, making in impossible for me to escape a third blow to my back.

Unable to get up off the floor, I kept rolling over and over even though that too, sent a sharp pain up my back. I was at least able to move enough to avoid the next blow. Under a pile of my clothes, about six feet in front of me, I could see the very end of Claude's pistol barrel peeking out.

I scratched and clawed my way toward the gun as Claude continued to his work with the pipe. I reached out to grab the gun just as the pipe came down with a crushing blow to my back and the back of my head. The gun was in my hand, but all around me the darkness begin to gather, each breath was harder to take than the last. I was hanging on somewhere in the edge of consciousness when I felt some-one rolling me over to my back.

And then a gun fired.

Chapter Twenty-two

T he next few days are nothing but a haze in my memory. I remember waking up a few times only to be asked a lot of questions by people in white coats. I remember my mother talking to me and seeing Willie at her side, but I'm not sure if that really happened, or whether I might have dreamed it.

Then one morning I woke up with a clear mind. After a second or two I realized I was in a hospital. I tried to sit up, but there was too much pain for that. Instead I looked around the room as best I could without moving. Lying on a cot beside my bed was Willie. He did not look very comfortable, but he was asleep. I tried to call his name, but even that took an effort and caused a lot of pain.

"Willie," I said in not much more than a whisper. His eyes flashed wide-open.

"Hank? You awake?" he said.

"Don't answer that," he said after seeing that I was, in fact, awake. "I'll get the doctor." He rushed out into the hall and in a few seconds returned with a doctor and two nurses who immediately went to work on me.

After the preliminaries were out of the way, the doctor said, "Well, Mr. Henrie, you've got three broken ribs, a punctured lung, a gunshot wound in your leg, some pretty serious damage to your cornea, twelve stitches in your top lip, another twenty-eight in your bottom lip, and seventeen or eighteen stitches around your face, neck, back, and arms. I would really like to know how all this happened, but there seems to be plenty of people interested in hearing that, so I'll take a rain check."

I nodded by way of saying thank you.

"I've got you on some strong painkillers, but you're going to be fine. I'm going to need to keep you in here until your lung heals."

Again I nodded.

"You're already tired, but I'm going to give you something to help you sleep better," he said and I could see the nurse injecting something into my IV. A few seconds later I drifted back to sleep.

The next time I woke up I felt considerably better. Looking around the room I saw my mother and Willie.

"How do you feel, son?" my mother said after seeing my eyes open.

"Better," I said as Willie got up to get the doctor. Five minutes later, they had checked me out and were gone again. My mother held my hand and caressed my face as she asked me how I felt and what I needed. Big tears welled up in her eyes as she talked. I could tell that she had so many questions about what had happened to me in the last week or so. She had been so worried. But she realized those questions would have to wait and she would have to rely on her faith in me for a little while longer until all the questions could be answered.

After an hour or so, sensing I think, that Willie and I needed to talk, she excused herself for the night saying that she would be back first thing in the morning. She gently placed a teary kiss on my forehead and left.

"I hate to do this to you, but we got some work to do," Willie said after my mother was gone.

"Let's get to it," I said.

"Well first of all, Suzanna is in the Leon County Jail. Atlanta PD is just letting her cool her heels down there while they figure out what happened. Locked away in jail here in Atlanta are Robert H. Simmons a.k.a. Cummings and two French people, a man and a woman who are claiming diplomatic immunity. A third Frenchman was dead, found lying on top of you with a bullet through his head in a warehouse about fifteen miles from here."

"Who shot the guy they found on me?" I said.

"They tell me you did. Found you unconscious with a gun in your hand."

I had no memory of it.

"What now?" I asked.

"Well, the Atlanta PD, FBI, and CIA are all itching to get their hands on you. Looks like they've got enough to clear you of the murder already, but I negotiated a blanket immunity deal for you anyway. You know, to cover any other crimes you may have committed along the way," he said with a smile.

"I don't want any deals. I'll tell them whatever they want to know," I said.

"You better be careful, Hank. This whole thing began with a breaking-and-entering," he said.

"I'll take my chances on that. They can prosecute if they want to."

The next few weeks were painful. Not just my recovery but the whole process of sorting out what had happened. The FBI and the CIA were not tipping their hand at all as they asked very specific questions about what happened, and Cummings's role in it all.

For my part I answered their questions as honestly and as fully as I could. The Atlanta PD were really only concerned about Stan's murder. I told them about what Cummings had told me about Sammy "The Grinder" Gritton.

But after only a few interviews with them, they closed their investigation at the request of the CIA and FBI citing national security concerns.

To this day the murder of Stansfield Tanner is technically "unsolved" and remains open. However, Willie's contact inside the FBI has told him that the FBI believes that Cummings did in fact hire Sammy "The Grinder" Gritton to take Stan out. Sammy's body was eventually found at the bottom of a northern Louisiana bayou, apparently the victim of a Mob hit. That too can probably be laid at the feet of Robert Simmons, or as he was known to me, Lester Cummings.

Chapter Twenty-three

It wasn't until months later, when Willie and I compared notes, that we pieced together what we thought was the actual story of what happened that week in October.

Early the following March, before the mosquitoes got too bad, Willie and I were sitting out on my dock late one afternoon.

"You saw where Robert Simmons was sentenced today?" Willie said.

"Yeah, life without parole. Must've really had a tight case against him to get him to plead guilty to life without parole," I said.

"Murder is a capital offense in Georgia," he said.

"You think they threatened to charge him with Stan's murder?" I said.

"Probably just enough to get a plea bargain on the rest of their case," Willie said.

"Well, the Feds can be tough," I said with a smile, hoping that they had bluffed Cummings into taking a bad deal.

"There is one thing I've never been able to figure out about this whole mess," Willie said.

"What?"

"If Cummings was working for the French Intelligence, why didn't they refuse to meet you at the airport and just let you give the disk to Cummings? If they'd done that, they could have killed you at the swap and popped Suzanna any time they wanted to. Case closed," Willie said.

"I've thought a lot about that, too. One reason is he probably never had the hard evidence on Gritton. Cummings had to know I would insist on seeing the evidence before I told him where the disk was," I said and then continued after a little more thought, "or maybe, Cummings had some reason for insisting that it be that way. He told me in the car at the airport that he wanted to keep working for the CIA, so maybe he refused to do it that way—insisted they try to make the swap themselves and he would only step in if he had to. That could have been the deal," I said.

"And that way if you had given them the disk, he simply checks in with the Chief of Security as he leaves the airport, tells him it was a false alarm and thanks for the help. They're none the wiser, neither is the CIA, and he has his big payday," Willie said.

"That's right, then I would either get in some kind of 'accident,' "—I said using my fingers to indicate quotation marks around the word "accident"—"or Cummings would have encouraged the FBI to arrest me for Stan's murder, which would have completely destroyed all my credibility. No one would have believed a word I said. Especially some wild story about a French spy ring."

" 'Course, you may have had more leverage than you think. The Feds have done a pretty good job of sweeping this thing under the rug. They may have let you off the hook just to keep the accusations from surfacing. I loved how they just let those French guys declare diplomatic immunity and fly away to Paris," Willie said.

I considered that for a minute before I said, "Yeah, and clamped that gag order on me."

"And about the only thing they've said about Stan's murder is that you weren't in on it," he said.

"How long do you think they will let Suzanna twist in the wind?" I said.

"My guy at the FBI said they might never take her off the suspect list. Which is fine with me. Might be the only punishment she gets in this whole thing," he said.

"Well, that's not insignificant. Going around the rest of your life, everybody thinking you might have gotten away with murder. It's not much of a lifestyle," I said.

"The other thing I can't figure in this whole thing is who she was working for," Willie said.

"You think it might have been the Chinese government?" I said.

"Why them?"

"You remember the week between Christmas and New Year's when they expelled those Chinese diplomats from the U.S.?" I said.

"Yeah."

"I wonder if it wasn't over this whole thing. They never offered any kind of official statement, they just sent them home."

"Could be right. She and Paul could have cut a deal with them. I never thought of it at the time, but that could be right," Willie said.

"The thing that haunts me most about the whole thing is Harrison Seppi. I have never found out exactly what happened to him," I said.

"Probably lost his job like the rest of the people on that disk. I imagine that's about it," Willie said.

"For a while I wondered if he had been killed. I had O'Malley do some quiet checking to see if he could find out anything, but he assured me he was alive and well. He thinks the Feds have him and his wife in a witness relocation program somewhere," I said.

"Probably all a distant memory to him now. Don't you think?" Willie said.

"I don't know. I imagine that night will stay fresh in his mind for a long, long time."

Epilogue

Later that summer I received an anonymous cashier's check for twenty-five thousand dollars drawn on CayBank. I had to laugh at the irony of Suzanna using that bank to send me the rest of the money she felt she owed me.

I kept the check under a magnet on my refrigerator for a few days and thought over what I should do with it. It was tempting, but in the end . . .

Are you kidding me? Of course I cashed it. I *earned* that money.